NINE MINUTES

By
Jacqueline Druga

Nine Minutes - Jacqueline Druga

Nine Minutes - Copyright 2019 by Jacqueline Druga

This is a work of fiction. Names, characters, places and incidents are either the product of the author's imagination or are used fictitiously, and any resemblance to any person or persons, living or dead, events or locales is entirely coincidental.

I put my 'thank you for your help' right here and I truly mean it when I say it. Thank you to Paula, Kira and Connie N for all your help!.

Covers courtesy of Red Ninja Designs

NINE MINUTES

ONE – BURGERS

Seventeen cities were incinerated within seconds while I served a hungry patron a bacon blue burger. Millions of people lost their lives in an instant while I and everyone else in the restaurant were oblivious to what was happening.

In a world where technology was a curse, for the longest time, the eatery where I worked was a blessing. It was praised when it opened. The Millicents were a couple in their eighties, one child, and they had hit the Pennsylvania lottery. Never caring if they took a loss, really wanting to fulfil their dream, since they had the windfall of money, they opened the PEF. The Peaceful, Easy Feedary. The name was a tribute to the Eagles, a band they both loved back in the day. When they interviewed me, they told me they wanted to hire me even before they met me simply because of my first name.

Henley.

I guess they assumed I was named after a band member.

"With such a unique name," Mrs. Millicent asked me, "I have to ask, were your parents Eagles fans?"

I didn't have the heart to tell her I wasn't named after the famed singer, but rather a style of shirt that my father was wearing when he met my mother.

Hating to admit, I was leery about taking the job at a new place. I had been waiting tables for twenty years, was good at what I did and used to making money. But the eatery was two blocks from my apartment.

The premise of it spread like wildfire and people made reservations for dinner weeks in advance, lunch time not so much.

It was a step back to the days when life was simple. When you went out to eat without the distraction of a television blaring in the corner, or your date playing with his or her phone.

All phones were turned in at the door.

The music wasn't on the radio, but a soothing choice by the owners.

All of that fed into the fact that the world began its descent while five staff members and twenty late afternoon diners had their lunch break. Talking away to each other with no distractions.

It was the one time there needed to be.

We were in the cultural section of town. A little city within the big, and even though it was an urban setting, there was very light traffic during the day.

I wasn't crazy about the area when we moved there. I stayed away from living in the city, there was something about it that I hated. I had been self-sufficient my whole adult life. When my daughter was born, I was single, but I wasn't a kid, I was a woman who kept rolling along.

I met my husband when Macy was just two, and for the first time ever in my life I let someone else make decisions.

That was a mistake.

After a few years of putting his artwork secondary to providing, he wanted to focus on his art and needed that artsy feel to be inspired to create his paintings. Bloomfield, PA, was his muse. Or so he said. I didn't get it. We were so out of place, having moved from the suburbs. We weren't city people, not at all. Even though I was always living check to check, I was a snob when it came to city schools and I sent Macy to Saint Mary's. She was in the first grade when we moved there, with rent it would be tight, but we'd manage.

Then Todd sold the painting of a lifetime. Before we knew it, he was on display at the museum, had lined up art show after art show, and left me for his business manager, Karen.

It was me and Macy alone ... again.

We just kinda stayed in that apartment. The building was nice, an old, three story Victorian style row house with eight units and neighbors that cared.

They cared. Yet, did they care enough about my daughter to check on her in the middle of the madness?

God, I hoped so. That was my first thought when I heard what was going on.

My poor child, nine years old, not only would I not be there when she got off the bus, I wouldn't be there to calm her or answer her questions.

It was a rare that I wasn't there. That was why I worked the lunch shift.

Lunch was usually over before three and I'd make it home just in time to greet her bus.

But on that day we had a late lunch group, an eight top as we referred to them. All men, they came in all ordering specialty burgers, onion rings and assorted appetizers.

I was never getting out of there; they were never finishing.

Margot worked behind the bar, she hated it, but she did it for an hourly wage plus small tip outs from the wait staff, until she took the floor for the dinner shift.

She leaned against the cooler, her auburn hair pulled into a ponytail, which draped over her left shoulder while she looked at her watch. I was looking at mine, too. *Yeah, could the day go any slower?*

After checking on my last remaining table's progress, I walked over to the bar.

"Can you take that table and finish it?" I asked Margot. "You can have the tip. I don't care. I just want to get home to greet the bus."

"That's a big tip," She looked over my shoulder to the men. "Didn't you say you had that old lady across the hall to watch out for Macy?"

I nodded. "I do, but I just hate having to rely on her. Especially if I can get home. Besides, Macy hates when I'm not there."

Mumbling a "sure," Margot did that 'whatever' eye roll. *Was she serious? She was staying anyhow, she had the next shift.*

She couldn't take that table?

"You know what?" I said. "Forget about it."

"Hen..."

"No. Don't worry about it." I walked away thinking the entire time, wait until she needed me. I got my bearings, not wanting my mood to affect my service. I took in the music. It was actually pretty cool, modern day music transformed into elevator tunes.

Once more I assessed my table of eight. One guy was almost done, the other talked so much he barely ate. Maybe he'd take it to go.

Meeting lunches at our place always went long. No one was checking their mail or sending texts, nor hiding their phone under the table as they sneakily tried to check it.

There was always one. At least once or twice a day someone cheated and kept their phone.

I was glad at that moment someone did.

Crash!

The sound of a breaking glass brought silence to the room, just before Margot let out an "Oh my God." She said it again, only faster and running the words together. "Oh my God, oh my God."

She looked down at her watch, looked at me, then her watch again. She hurriedly grabbed her purse and rushed from behind the bar.

Her watch. It wasn't a normal one. It was one that connected to your phone and the internet.

One of the patrons jokingly said, "Wow, someone is ready to go home."

Laughter. Laughter. Ha, ha, ha.

"Margot?" I called out to her. "Everything okay?"

She paused at the door. Her lips moved for a few second before words came out. "Go home, we're at war." She spun and ran out.

9

TWO – UNLOCK

There was a delayed reaction in the room, people dismissing what she said, then almost like a switch, something clicked.

"She can't be serious," one of the patrons said. "Who the hell are we at war with?"

"Anyone," another answered. "Think about it."

"Something big happened," someone said. "She wouldn't react like that otherwise."

My head was going back and forth, trying to process what Margot said. Chef and Cook flew from the kitchen, repeating Margot's advice to go home. Then the other waitress left the floor, and instantly our quiet little haven was a madhouse.

"What's going on?"

"Does anyone have their phone? Someone check their phone."

"Get me my phone." A man grabbed the tops of my arms as if to shake me from my frozen stance.

"Yes, yes, okay." I was muttering in confusion. It was hard to actually figure out what was going on. Margot declaring we were at war, what did that even mean?

"Now!" someone screamed in my face, causing me to jump.

I spun and ran behind the check in counter.

It wasn't that easy. The phones and electronic devices weren't placed in a bin. Our system worked like a coat check system. Everyone was given a ticket with a number and tiny key. Instead of a line of hangers, we had a wall, five foot tall with rows of what looked like safety deposit boxes. It was only twenty people, but it was insane. At least eight of those customers were in the same box.

I lifted the first tag and key tossed to me.

219.

Box number 219.

I scanned with my eyes looking for that box, but I didn't see it. Maybe it was my nerves, people screaming at me to hurry. My body trembled and I just wanted them all to shut up, they weren't making it better or easier.

"Find box seven."

"Our phones are in one-eleven."

"Sixty-four, right there. Right there! Can't you see it? What the hell is the matter with you!"

"Hurry up!"

I kept thinking *my God, just stop, the world isn't going to explode.*

Unfortunately, my way of thinking was way off.

It had already begun to explode.

Just at my breaking point, where I wanted to cover my ears with both hands and scream, it dawned on me.

The release.

There was a simple release, a one key, one turn, that opened the entire covering to the boxes, drawer doors and all. It was designed to enable us to get to a phone in case a key to a locked box was lost.

"Wait," I called out. "I got it. I know what to do."

I opened the cash drawer, pulled out the keys, sought the correct one and with shaking hands, unlocked the safety box unit.

The door swung open exposing small bins in what looked like mail slots.

I didn't know what bin was which number, and I just started pulling them. If they had a phone, I tossed it on the counter.

I was robotic and just kept moving. Grab a box, set it on the counter. Get another box ... empty. Empty ... phones.

I could hear them behind me fighting over devices, but I didn't care, I didn't look at them. I just wanted to get in the back, get my purse and phone and go.

The commonly used phrase, 'Oh my God' was repeated in different stages of emotion. Anger, sadness and shock.

People talked about war, asking how it was possible. With

each comment I heard my heart beat faster. Once the last box was pulled and the last phone set out, I didn't look back, I went straight to the kitchen and to my locker to grab my purse.

Hurriedly, I grabbed my phone and turned it on.

"Come on, come on, come on," I beckoned it to power up faster.

When it powered on, I saw the time of 2:45. And I clicked to access the internet.

Surely, if war broke out, if something truly big did happen, it would be on a news site.

Even using my phone's data didn't help the internet open, it was slow, as was the news website. Those twenty or thirty seconds seemed like an hour. Finally, the news opened up and I didn't need to search for anything. The headline was bold and huge. It was frightening and real, it took my breath away.

Paris Burns – Millions Dead.

THREE – GATHER

It was headline after headline as I scrolled down. I had to stop looking, but it was like a part of me needed to know as much as I could before walking out the door.

All words.

Stock pictures.

Where were the images?

Paris Burns

Six Countries Hit

Global Confrontation Erupts.

Those were the words I saw but no answers.

Who started it? When did it start? Why did it start? Jesus, wasn't that the foundation of good journalism? The who, what, where, when and how? Shouldn't those be answered almost immediately?

Deep inside, maybe it was wishful thinking, for a split second I imagined it wasn't in my country. That it was elsewhere. That somehow, the 'we're at war' that Margot muttered wasn't really about us. Until I saw it.

New York.

It was hit.

I didn't look any further to see where else. New York was close enough.

Nearly fumbling my phone, I shoved it in my purse, tossed the strap over my shoulder and grabbed my backpack that hung over the hook.

I was going to hightail it out of there, get my daughter and figure out what was going on. Were we safe or would we have to find a way out of the city? Because truth be known, if a bomb fell on the city, we were close enough to be toast.

I had to get things together and hit the road if needed. Be one of those panicked people who fled for the streets.

Just about out of the kitchen, I stopped.

I looked down to my watch. I had twenty minutes until Macy's bus got home, and two blocks to run.

Supplies.

Maybe it was wrong, maybe I was overreacting, who knew, but I unzipped my backpack. I thought about taking out that extra set of clothes and shoes in there, but I didn't, I crammed them in and raced about the kitchen grabbing what I could.

A can of this, a box of that. I forewent going down to the basement to the freezers. Not only was there not enough time, it was useless to take any of that. I went into the dry storage pantry, grabbed handfuls of crackers and what I could, until my bag was stuffed.

I hadn't a clue if it would be enough, I had food at home. All I kept thinking was I needed extra just in case the stores were looted or people went insane and chaotic.

Before shutting my bag, I saw it on the wall. The first aid box. I opened it, grabbed handfuls of items then finally shut my bag.

When I emerged into the main portion of the restaurant it was empty.

Through the windows I could see people moving quickly on the sidewalks. The normal light traffic was suddenly crammed to a halt on the main drag in front of the eatery.

Did they know something I didn't?

I was just going to go, run out of the store, instead I took a second. Being one of the few employees to have a key, I locked the door.

I didn't want anyone breaking in, stealing anything. Then again, was I any better? I just took from my place of employment.

I'd apologize profusely if I jumped the gun and acted irrationally, but I couldn't think about that right then, or even feel guilty.

I just had to get home.

FOUR - INFORM

There was an indescribable feeling of panic that hit me. My heart beating out of control, all thoughts of doom, I immediately, and ignorantly went into some sort of flight mode.

I ran all the way home. I didn't have a plan on what to do next, just grab my daughter and go. Where, I didn't know.

I wasn't thinking clearly, or rather, I wasn't doing any informed thinking. All I knew was a few words that I read on my phone and in my mind that was enough.

I barreled my way down the street bumping into people. Still wearing my apron, my tips must have flown out of my pocket. At one point, someone grabbed me to stop me and say I had dropped money.

I didn't care.

My focus was getting to the bus stop, grabbing my daughter and then leaving the city.

The entire time I ran, I struggled to catch my breath. I fought to not throw up and constantly looked at the sky waiting for the bombs to fall.

I lived on a busy side street. The houses were all row houses, all old, big and connected. Macy's bus stop was on the corner, a half block from our building. I thought briefly about running up to the apartment, grabbing my car keys, and just shoving her in the car and going. There wasn't time, I could see her bus in the distance.

As I drew closer to my building, I saw another obstacle. A pick-up truck was double parked on the street in front of my building. Not only that he was blocking in my car.

Already out of breath and frightened of the unknown, I could feel a 'freak out' mode stewing and growing inside of me.

I didn't have time to blast whoever it was for blocking me in, that would come after I got Macy.

Running by my building, eyes transfixed only on the

nearing bus, I slammed into a guy carrying a box.

The connection sent the box from his hands to the ground, and my feet stumbled into them, causing me to spin and, like that box, toppling to the ground.

"Whoa. Whoa. Hey, you okay?" he asked, reaching down to help me.

It was the new guy moving in on my floor, I had seen him two days earlier.

"Yeah." That heavy backpack threw my balance off some, and I swayed as I stood. "Yeah. I am." I tried to get away.

"What's the rush?"

That inner freak out feeling, the one brewing inside of me erupted, and uncontrollably, I blasted him. "The bombs are coming. Didn't you hear the news?"

I believe I might have growled or maybe called him a bad name, but it didn't matter, I wasn't thinking. I ran to the corner just as the bus pulled up.

That out of control, panicked and confused feeling instantaneously lifted the second I saw my daughter step from the bus and say, "Hi, Mommy."

She smiled innocently, unaware of what was going on.

It was at that moment I knew the way I acted and felt was unacceptable. I had to get it together, I had to … for her.

◇◇◇◇

Our apartment wasn't much. It was small. The building manager told me the main area was called an open floor plan. It looked to me like one large room where they created a kitchen by building one of those half walls with a counter on it to divide the area. Behind the kitchen was a short hall that led to the two bedrooms and a bathroom where the tub touched the toilet. Macy's room was a glorified walk in closet, but she liked it and it didn't take much to convince her to go to her room.

I needed her out of the way so I could immerse myself with the news. I made her a quick mac and cheese, gave her my phone and let her play.

Of course, she griped because the internet was slow.

I sat close to the television, volume down, close captions on. Did I think my daughter could handle the news? Absolutely she could. I just couldn't handle explaining anything until I had all the facts.

Sadly, facts were hard to come by.

I flipped station to station, and they all said the same thing.

The six countries hit were all the usual war suspects. US, UK, Russia, China, India and even North Korea

It didn't make sense, who was doing the bombing? Obviously, it was a country not hit. But which country really had those capabilities?

There were seventeen cities in all. In the United States, Houston, Chicago, Los Angeles and New York. They reported three weapons went off in New York alone, as if one wasn't enough. Moscow was hit with four.

Since the blanket of strikes, nothing else had occurred. I supposed it was a good sign.

Still, there were no true answers or images, although they kept announcing they'd have satellite or drone footage shortly.

Did I really want to see it?

I was engrossed in listening to experts rehash the same thing on different networks, just phrased differently. I kept flipping channels, as if I would luck out and catch the big information by chance.

I was so into listening that the knock on my door made me jump in my seat. Eyes still on the television, ears tuned in to what they were saying, I walked to the door and peered out the peephole.

It was the new guy, the one I bumped into.

I opened the door.

"Hey," he said.

It was the first time I ever really looked at him. I had seen him here and there. He was maybe late thirties or forty, average height, so I didn't have to look up to him. Which was a good thing, he seemed intimidating. His brown hair needed combed and he had a face that looked like he never smiled.

Surely, he was there to lambaste me for breaking something in one of his boxes.

"Hey," I replied, then shifted my listening focus back to the television.

"I'm the guy moving into 2C."

"Oh, yeah, I know, listen about ..."

"Are you okay?"

"Huh?" I asked.

"I was just seeing if you were okay," he said.

"Oh, yeah, just a brush burn on my hand." I held it up. "Fine."

"No, I mean, about all that's going on with ..."

He said something further, but I didn't listen because all I heard was the announcement that the president was about to speak.

"Shit. I have to go," I said hurriedly. "Thanks for asking. The president's on."

I shut the door, not thinking anymore about my interaction with 2C and raced to the couch.

I don't know what I was expecting to hear.

He started his speech about the horrendous acts of the day, how devastating they were for the country and the world, and it would take a lot of fortitude to get through it.

He assured the American public that we were not in a state of war and there wasn't a global confrontation. I wasn't comforted by that, I barely believed that, after all, seventeen cities across the world had been flattened.

In the two minutes and forty-three seconds he was on the air, the president urged calm, pleaded for people not to panic shop, said he was confident it was over and would return when he had concrete information to give.

That was it.

No indication of why it happened or who was behind it.

It was a 'wait and see' situation, and I had to resolve myself that I would have to do just that. Wait by the television and see.

FIVE - RANSOM

The news had to wait. I turned it off when Macy grew tired of staying in her room. She played video games for a while after we had a sandwich for our meal.

She asked me what was wrong, what was going on.

I was honest that I didn't have answers and that there was maybe something very bad happening.

I asked her to trust me and that I would do anything to keep her safe.

While the powers that be contemplated what they would tell the public, I didn't sit idly.

I tried calling what little bit of family I had. My cousin in Denver, uncle in Toledo, anyone I could think of. All of them told me to be calm.

I listened to the experts on what to pack in something called a bug out bag. I broke out a notepad and took notes. I had my backpack and a small duffle bag, and I loaded not only with what I had, but conceivably could carry.

The news and expert guests reiterated over and over that the threat was over. While it was beyond tragic what happened, we wouldn't see anymore.

The world had been brought to a standstill, but it wasn't the apocalypse.

That's what they said.

After I got Macy to bed, I looked for places to go. Where would we be safe? I needed a destination.

My first thought was to go south to West Virginia. The hills and woods would be a safe haven. I located a KOA campsite deep in the state and only a two and a half hour drive from my home.

Obviously, I wasn't the only person thinking about getting out of the cities. My ten PM phone call was actually answered, and I was told they had been selling spots left and right, they had nothing.

I pleaded with the man and eventually he told me to come on down, he had a pup tent and a small spot he could let me have.

I wasn't sure what that was, but if I was away from populated areas, I was safe.

I would leave the next morning.

Others were taking it as serious as I was. At least more serious than the news. Maybe they were trying to quell panic. Common sense told me seventeen cities hit by nuclear weapons wasn't the end of the events, it had to be the beginning.

And I was right.

Just after midnight, after I finished putting the last of the items in my bag and felt good about my plan, they broke the news to the public on what was happening.

The Director of Homeland security along with the Secretary of Defense held a late night news conference. They stated the facts without emotions, telling us they waited to release the information so they could answer any and all possible questions.

"Confidence is high," the Homeland Director said. "Nothing further will occur, rest assured, we have an alternate plan. Details of that will be released in the morning."

Then the Secretary of Defense returned to the podium to talk more and answer questions.

It wasn't a global confrontation. One country didn't declare war on another. It was a mastermind terrorist plot that was at least ten years in the making.

An impenetrable computer virus had invaded the defense system of every technological country with nuclear capabilities.

"It disguised itself as a working system," The secretary explained. "Until we realized what had happened, then it was too late."

A reporter asked, "Why did we not see them coming?"

"It disguised itself as a working system," the Secretary repeated. "Nothing appeared on our radar until the bombs reached their destination. At that point, the virus locked us out."

"What do you mean locked you out?"

"We can't access the system at this time to shut it down or launch an interception. Our SLBM launch systems are not affected. Unfortunately, there aren't enough of those to have an effective interception rate should the threat be carried out."

The threat.

The threat wasn't the initial seventeen, they were a warning.

This massive conglomerate, or a terror organization, had given their demands.

They not only wanted exuberant amounts of money and resources, they wanted land, territories, leadership, recognition and power.

If they did not receive confirmation that their demands would be met, the remaining global nuclear arsenal would be released.

We had forty-eight hours.

They urged people to remain calm, that the best minds in the world were working on cracking the virus and they were certain they would.

I felt vulnerable and scared. I cried for a good hour and just wanted to grab Macy, get in my car and run for the hills. However, as I watched the news unfold, people took to the streets in chaos, rioting and looting.

Grabbing what they could. Fighting others as if they were the villains when we should have been helping each other.

Drone footage was released of the cities that were hit, the images of the burnt and ruined cities seared into my soul. I wished I hadn't looked.

The streets were chaotic while the panel of four experts on the news were composed, yet honest.

"There's nowhere to go, really," said Panel One member said. "Stay in the cities and die fast or leave and die slowly. The outcome is the same."

"I think they'll crack it," Panel Two said.

"There should be a plan B," added Panel Member Three.

"Find another way just in case."

"They are," replied Panel Four. "They just haven't told us yet."

"I'm not talking about the people and a survival plan," said Panel Three. "I'm talking about an alternative solution to the virus."

Panel One laughed. "Like what?"

"Manually dismantle the bombs," Panel Three said. "If they haven't already started."

Panel Four chuckled. "That's three thousand warheads."

"Start now," said Panel Three. "They win either way. They don't give a damn about the destruction, they'd die for their cause. So ... If we don't crack the virus, don't dismantle, there is only one other alternative."

"And that is?" asked Panel One.

"Give them what they want."

We were at an impasse. Listening to the so-called experts, the politicians, didn't enlighten me or encourage me.

All I knew was, we had two days.

In two days we'd find out our fate.

SIX – CONTEMPLATION

Sleep wasn't easy. Especially once I realized that the forty-eight hour warning started when the first wave of bombs landed. It took my body going into shut down mode, and I went from counting down the minutes until the emergency plan was announced to waking up to the sound of ambulances.

Instantly I shot into panic mode again. I jumped up, sirens blaring, on top of the steady sound of helicopters.

Not wanting to scare Macy, I washed up, had some coffee and calmed myself. I had to be calm. The bombs had not come yet, and if we were a designated hit site, which I believed we were, I still had thirty-two hours. Thirty-two hours to get far away from the city and out of range.

Every map they showed on the news as potential fallout areas, had West Virginia as one of the least.

My choice was a wise one.

I wasn't sure what kind of mayhem I would run into on the road. I guessed it would be bad. A lot of people would leave.

At least I knew I had plenty of gas. I had used up my fuel perks a couple days before, the discount on gas earned from grocery shopping. I'd make it to west Virginia and farther if needed.

After I had my coffee and my wits restored, I thought it would be best to take our things down to my car. I had them ready by the door.

As I was about to, the sound of another chopper flying overhead startled me.

What was going on?

The sirens were continuous.

"Mommy?" Macy called my name. She stood in the small hall, all sleepy eyed. "What's all the noise?"

"I don't know baby."

"Did you watch the news?"

I shook my head. I wasn't going to watch the news anymore. It didn't matter what the government had planned, I was leaving and could listen in the car. "No, we're gonna go."

"To school?'

"No, we're ..." I forced a smile. "Camping. We're going camping."

"What do we know about camping?"

"Absolutely nothing, but hey ..." I walked to her and kissed her on the forehead. "It's not too late to learn."

She giggled and smiled.

"Hey, why don't you get dressed."

"Where are you going?"

"I'm gonna take our stuff down to the car."

"Okay." She nodded. "Do I need to wear anything special for camping?"

"Just jeans."

"Then will you tell me what's going on?" She asked.

"I will in the car. I promise."

"It's bad, mom, isn't it?"

"It could be, sweetie, it could be."

I waited until she turned and walked down the hall. She paused when the sirens blasted loudly, as if right by our house.

Grabbing the bags, I opened the door.

I didn't hear any voices in the halls or stairs. As I carried my things, I kept thinking about how silly I probably looked. Like one of those families in the movies that pack up their station wagon and hurriedly leave town as if the apocalypse was better elsewhere.

It had to be, right? The safe scenario had to be anywhere there wasn't any cities or military bases.

Weighted down with the two backpacks and duffel bag, I made my way outside. I didn't know what to expect. With the blaring sounds of sirens and loud helicopter noises, I expected outside to be a war zone. Something big had happened, a riot, fire, something. Whatever was causing the noise was just a reinforcement that I needed to get out of the city as soon as possible.

My street seemed quiet, it was early morning, but that was briefly. As soon as I stepped to the sidewalk, a car zoomed in reverse down my street. Just as he passed me, he stopped, screeching tires, he spun in a turnaround, ramming his back end into a parked car. After the impact he peeled down the road.

Thinking it was a sign of the insanity, I went to my car. It was close to the door of my building. I unlocked the doors and reached for the back handle.

"If you're trying to get out and leave the city, don't bother," he said

I turned to my left to see 2C approaching. He carried a large backpack as he walked toward me.

"What?" I asked.

"I said, if you're trying to get out of the city. If you're trying to leave. Don't bother. I just tried."

"You just moved to the area," I said. "Maybe you don't know all the ways. I lived here a while. I know all the ways out."

"It's useless. You won't get far."

I shook my head and opened the car door. After tossing in the bags, I shut the door. "I'm going to try."

"Okay. Your choice. You'll fail," he said.

"Why would you say that?"

"Because there is a ban on all civilian vehicles on the road."

"What did he just say?" A male voice asked from behind me.

I looked over to my right, the man in apartment 1B stood there.

"I was telling her there is a civilian vehicle ban," 2C repeated. "It's in effect until midnight. I didn't know this until, well, I went out."

"What does that mean?" 1B asked. I had seen 1B around the building a lot. Never really gotten too much into a conversation with him. He was older, probably retired, and was always carrying a grocery bag. He'd smile at me with a nod, but that was about it for our interaction.

With a hint of sarcasm, I answered, "I believe it means that no civilian vehicles are allowed on the road."

1B laughed. "How do they enforce that?"

"Tell you to turn around," 2C replied.

"They can't have every road blocked," I said. "No way. There has to be a way around, I know there is."

2C lifted his hands. "That's what I thought. If you don't believe me. Go look. We're literally a half a block from craziness."

It probably wasn't the best parenting move, considering my daughter was up in the apartment alone and asleep, but I had to see. Arms folded, I walked down to the corner to where she caught her bus.

It was an intersection, to my right, I saw traffic, and when I looked to my left where I could catch a glimpse of the main drag, I saw what 2C was talking about.

Police lights flashed, traffic was crammed at the intersection, even if they could be on the street, moving was impossible.

"Stop!" I heard a male voice call out. "Why are you doing this?"

A young man was slightly resisting arrest. They had him handcuffed from behind, pulling him.

"Why are you taking me?" he asked in an angry plea. "I didn't do anything. I didn't do anything. Stop. Please. Let me go."

Both officers pulled him toward the massive amount of traffic, probably to one of the squad cars.

I saw enough, turned and went back.

"Well?" 2C asked.

"Okay, it's crazy."

"I tried," 2C said. "I pulled up a map of the area and everything. Went side streets. They still got me. They warn you to turn around. If you don't, they disable your vehicle."

"They won't disable the vehicle," I scoffed.

"Yeah, they do. I know," 2C said. "They disabled mine."

"For real?" I asked shocked. "How?"

"Shot my tires."

"Until midnight, you say?" 1B asked. "Did they say why?'

2C shook his head. "No, but I looked on my phone. They are evacuating all hospitals and care facilities first."

That made sense with all the helicopters and sirens. We lived a few blocks from three different hospitals.

"Swell," 1B said. "It's the apocalypse and only the sick and old will survive."

"Really?" I shook my head at him, then looked to 2C. "How about foot traffic? Are we allowed to walk?"

"You really want to walk?" he asked. "Think about it, you'll have to walk out of the red and orange zones, then try to find a place that is safe once you get out and for a while. My only option now is to get an evac bus. They'll at least get me out of the area and to a safe zone."

"Where?" I asked. "Where are they going?"

"As far as I can tell, yellow zone or lighter. Public buildings, garages." He shrugged. "If I go on foot, I won't get into one of those places, and I don't know anyone in the other zones I could call."

"Wait. Wait. Wait." I held up my hand. "Zones?"

"Yeah, I printed it this morning when WPXI posted it." He unfolded a sheet of paper and handed it to me. I looked at the map of our city. It looked Ike a target map with rings of different colors, black was center, red was around that and we were in the outer section of orange. "What does this mean?"

"Black means, well, you know what that means. The red is blast and fire, the orange is blast damage. Those three areas instant death is imminent. So, it's important to get out of those areas."

"And we can't do it until midnight?" I asked.

2C shook his head. "And that's if they don't change that."

"Okay," I sighed out. "I guess I'll wait until then."

"What about you?" 1B asked 2C. "They disabled your car. What are you gonna do?"

"Like I said, take the evacuation bus. They're supposed to announce pick ups and schedules."

"Well, if you want a ride, you can leave with me," 1B said. "I have no problem with that.

'Thank you, I appreciate that." 2C said with a nod.

I went back to my car and grabbed my bags. I wasn't leaving our supplies out there. I wished both of them good luck and headed back into the building. I had the blast map to print up, double check my route and be ready to roll as soon as the clock struck twelve.

It was later than I wanted to leave, but what choice did I have? Walking made no sense, especially after listening to what 2C said.

Leaving at midnight still gave me fourteen and a half hours to get twenty or so miles.

Plenty of enough time.

I was confident.

The remaining time before I could go had to be well spent. The first thing I did upon returning to my apartment was turn on the news and a double check about the civilian vehicle ban.

2C wasn't wrong.

It was indeed in effect.

I explained to Macy what was going on as best as I could, trying not to scare her, but keeping things realistic.

"Is it going to really happen, Mom?" She asked.

"I hope not," I told her. "But we have to act as if it would."

When thinking about it, was it really going to occur? Would the powers that be, the leaders of billions of people allow a total nuclear annihilation to happen? I just couldn't see it.

The network news channels ran constantly. Retired Military personnel were reassuring that while it could go down to the last minute, it wasn't going to happen. That they were probably already dismantling many of the weapons.

All well and fine I thought, that was in the United States, I was pretty sure those weren't the weapons coming our way.

In my heart I didn't think it would happen.

I didn't feel it or 'see' it. Not that I was a psychic, but when faced with something that was supposed to happen, if I couldn't see it happening, it wasn't going to happen.

A weird gut instinct.

On this, I had to prepare even though I didn't feel we were going to face the bombs.

I mean, we could look like fools. If we did, the local news station was going to look the same.

They promised to continue broadcasting as long as possible, but were set up remotely in a safe zone. They reported areas outside of the city that were helping people and areas that were dangerous.

Even though they kept stating that the situation would resolve, every station continuously spoke of survivor tips. What to do, what not to do.

I didn't know how they knew all this information. We had never been in an all out nuclear conflict.

There was no real basis other than Hiroshima and Nagasaki, and both of those weapons were tiny compared to what we faced.

The news made sure to show a visualization.

And it wouldn't be just one bomb. In bigger cities, it was two or three.

It was insane.

I was ready.

I had my bug out bags filled with my supplies. I had that blast map, and a list of shelters to go to if for some reason I didn't make it to West Virginia. In fact, I printed up several blast maps of nearby areas they thought would be hit.

If I had any questions about post nuclear war, I went online. While the electricity was still on, I charged my phone and two power banks.

At ten minutes to twelve I would go sit it my car with my daughter, ready to go when the ban was lifted.

If indeed it turned out to be real, if the virus wasn't beaten, if the bombs were still coming, I would clear of the orange area long before they fell.

With my designation of West Virginia, hell, I'd not only be out of the orange ... I'd be in the clear.

SEVEN – BUG OUT

'The lifting of the civilian vehicle ban seems to have sparked a frenzy. Authorities weren't expecting," the news reporter said over the radio. "An instant gridlock of traffic trying to flee the city has brought the remaining evacuation attempts to a halt."

No, shit, I thought.

I was tense. My hands gripped and released the wheel. As I sat in bumper to bumper traffic not three blocks from my home.

I hadn't moved in hours

I pulled out of the parking spot as soon as midnight hit, feeling confident until I hit the turn for the bridge. That was the problem with Pittsburgh. When you resided in an arm of the town, like I did in Bloomfield, you had to cross a bridge to really get anywhere. If I wanted to head north, I needed a bridge. My destination was south. I thought about going through Shadyside then Oakland, but I knew that would be worse. It was worse when there was a crisis.

I opted for the Bloomfield Street Bridge, the only problem with that was the route encircled the downtown area.

When I left at midnight, I thought I'd be clear of the city by then. As I sat in traffic with twelve hours to go, I worried. I couldn't move forward, backwards nor to my left or right. I was boxed in there.

Cars beeped their horns as if that was going to move traffic.

I switched the radio to try to hear something else. They talked about how there were no negotiations with the terrorist, and the governments were confident they'd crack the virus.

Russia assured the president they were taking measures to manually dismantle warheads, but no one really said how that task was going. I thought of it as a way to appease the public. Really it couldn't be easy to do that.

In my mind, the stubborn heads of state, unwilling to give

in to the terrorist, were sitting cozy in a bunker somewhere.

They didn't want to give up power or land, but in a sense, they were.

Macy was asleep in the back seat, leaning against the door.

I looked around at the cars and trucks around me, the drivers like me, sitting there, all with the same expressions.

Every now and again, you'd hear the crash of metal as someone tried to push their way through.

Another switch of the station.

'Port Authority transit and several school bus providers are dispatching more evacuation vehicles. Civilians are urged to use the buses as a means to leave the city. All available police and emergency personnel have been recalled and will be clearing a single lane for evacuation buses only in hopes to move traffic. The less civilian vehicles on the road the easier things will move along. They are asking people to be patient while they remove abandoned cars.'

They went on to name locations.

I understood the logic.

Get cars off the road, open it up to buses and things would flow.

That's was great in theory.

But would it work, and would it work in enough time?

It was a rotation of the same information. How to leave the city, evacuation stations, and what to do if you stay behind.

I had no intentions of staying behind. I was on my way out. I would get across that bridge.

Those dreams of escape were soon crushed when I noticed a family walking.

After them, more people walked.

At first, I couldn't figure out where they were coming from until I realized they were leaving their cars.

Just leaving them in the middle of traffic. Everyone behind them was unable to move any farther, and I was one of those people.

I knew at that moment, I had no other choice.

If I wanted out of the city and into some sort of safety zone, me and my daughter, like those in the line of traffic ahead of us, would have to also abandon our car and walk.

The car had already been in park, and I simply shut it off. I grabbed my backpack from the front seat, opened the passengers' door behind me and reached for the duffle bag.

"Mace," I called out to her.

She lifted her head.

"Come on baby." I held out my hand.

"Are we here?"

"No. We're still near home. We're gonna head to an evacuation station."

"We're just going to leave the car?" She grabbed my hand.

"Yeah, we are. We don't have a choice.

Once she locked her hand in mine, I made sure the duffle was adjusted over my shoulder, and I helped her out of the car.

It was crazy looking out into the sea of non-moving cars. It felt dangerous, like walking in traffic.

I needed to get us to one of those evacuation centers, it was my only option. Walk and pray that the crisis would be over.

I expected maneuvering through the cars with my daughter and belongings to be difficult, I didn't expect for people to get so angry and mean.

"Get back in your car!"

Beep. Beep.

"Thanks a fucking lot you bitch!"

They shouted horrible things at me and Macy, along with others that walked.

I kept her close to me as people grew ugly.

A man opened his door into me, hitting me in the side. Another inched his car our way.

"You okay?" A man asked, he was with his wife and two daughters.

"Yes. yes, thank you," I said.

"Follow us. Ignore them," he told me.

"We weren't getting off that bridge," his wife added. "They're clearing lanes for buses. That's the best bet."

I agreed, but didn't say anything. I just nodded.

I focused on walking in between the cars, I could handle being hit by a door, I could protect Macy from that. I just hoped no one shot at us or worse.

The man and his family moved at a quicker pace than us. They zig zagged in between cars, while Macy and I stayed straight.

"I'm scared," my daughter said.

"Me, too."

I wanted to shield her. I felt like we were in some sort of public stoning ceremony, where instead of rocks, they threw words and other items they could find.

"Almost out, pretty soon ..."

I saw it.

I didn't want to, it wasn't intentional, but I was watching the man and his wife.

The sights and sounds happened at the same time. A slight bang of metal against metal, that sounded like more of a fender bender, followed by a woman's horrifying scream.

I guess the wife inspired some sort of road rage as she tried to make her way between two vehicles.

The driver of the brown SUV rammed right into her. His front end cutting into her gut and pinning her to the back of the other SUV.

Her children saw this.

I grabbed Macy turning her into me so she wouldn't see.

The woman cried in pain, screaming out over and over, blood pouring from her mouth.

The driver of the brown SUV stepped out. I thought he was going to help her, apologize, break down, instead he pointed at her and said, "You're not going anywhere now, are you?" Then got back into his SUV. He backed up a little and her body fell limply. There wasn't enough room for her to hit the ground, instead she fell forward toward the hood of the SUV that hit her.

The driver? He sat in the driver's seat staring forward looking as if he was waiting in everyday rush hour and the woman was nothing but a hood ornament he had seen a dozen times.

The husband tried to help. The children cried.

Not a soul got out of their cars.

The bombs hadn't even fallen yet and we turned on ourselves.

I didn't want to think about what we'd become if the bombs did fall.

Keeping Macy's face buried against me, I made my way toward the man. "I'm sorry," I told him. "I'm so sorry."

He cried, trying to free his wife.

It was horrifying to watch, to know that those children would watch their mother die on a road, and people would just keep going.

I was just as bad.

I had my daughter to protect and for as much as I wanted to do something, there was nothing I could do but keep going and get Macy to an evacuation center.

Liberty Avenue was the main stretch of Bloomfield. It held most of the restaurants, including the one I worked. It had been sealed off a block from the intersection to the Bloomfield. When I drove, I had to take the side streets, which were jammed as well.

I imagined the reason for the blockade was traffic.

Six police cars were by the barricade, a couple had their lights flashing, a few looked abandoned.

My daughter seemed mesmerized by them and kept staring at the car.

"Mom," she called my name.

"Yeah, sweetie."

She said something like, 'do they know he's there' I'm not sure what her wording was, I placated her and told her yes as I focused on getting to West Penn and trying to shed the image out of my mind of that woman pinned between the vehicles.

It was heartbreaking to see and I felt guilty for walking away.

But I had my child to worry about, and I had to get her out of the city.

To my surprise, not only was the street beyond the barricade free of jammed traffic, it was lined with buses.

I smiled and emotionally laughed in relief. People were lined up waiting to board.

This was it, so simple, just get on a bus. Or so I thought, until I approached a line.

A fireman was moving the line along.

"Do we just pick a bus and get in line?" I asked him.

Before he answered me, I realized the answer was no. Those boarding the bus were showing him slips of papers, their bus tickets to salvation.

"Excuse me," I tried again. "Do we just get in line?"

"You have to get a bus slip at the hospital," he told me, checking passes as people boarded.

I thanked him and continued walking with Macy, it was a few blocks. But I was hopeful. The buses were lined up, waiting to go.

We took our spot in the long line of people, while the evacuation person instructed people to 'remain calm' there was room for everybody.

They'd probably fill the buses, wait for the lane to be free and then roll out.

I truly felt less desperate, seeing the buses and the organization Where the sound of smashing cars should have been frightening, it was a bright spot because I knew it was the sound of them moving the abandoned cars and clearing a lane.

Just before six am we made it through the line and received our bus assignment. We walked another block down the road to ours. There were buses behind it as well. A full scale caravan of buses.

We took our spot in line, waiting to board, and that was when I spotted 2C. He was ahead of me and was looking around.

He made eye contact with me. "Hey," he said.

I gave an upward nod of my head.

2C stepped from his place in line and joined me and Macy. "I thought you left a while ago?"

"Yeah, a lot of good that did. We couldn't get over the bridge."

"At least it sounds like they're clearing it," he commented.

"It does."

"We saw a woman get smashed," Macy blurted out. "Some guy just smashed her into another car."

2C blinked a few times in his surprise over hearing that. "Wow, seriously?"

Macy nodded. She projected as if she wasn't scared or fazed by it, I knew she was.

"It was horrifying," I replied. "What ... what happened to our neighbor? I thought you were going with him?"

"I did. He's on the first bus because of his age. Same problem as you. We were trying to go east, but there was no getting through."

He tried to keep making conversation, I didn't feel much like talking. I was exhausted and just wanted to get on the bus. Finally, they boarded us and 2C planted himself by us as well. I didn't get it. Maybe because I was the only one familiar to him.

It felt like they were pushing the time limit, because we didn't start to roll until ten-thirty. It was still four hours, but it felt like they were cutting it close. I thought perhaps something broke, maybe they cracked the virus and if they didn't, surely, they had a clear shot of getting us out.

We rode incredibly slow, a crawl down the street, but finally we were moving. I could see it was more than just our caravan of buses. As we approached the bridge a line of buses inched their way onto the cleared lane.

That had to be the reason it took so long to leave. They had a lot of clearing to do. I tried to survey what was ahead, pressing my head against the bus window to see out, but I couldn't.

Those on the bus went from chatty and relieved to tension you could feel as the bus barely crept along.

I kept telling myself, we're moving, that was a good thing.

The volume of voices was low, mixing it with the bus radio and the talk between the drivers. Passengers muttered words of concerns, asking the bus driver if the road was clear and would we make it out.

"They gave us the all clear," the bus driver replied. "Just a lot of buses and trucks in this lane moving people out like you."

It was a good explanation and people accepted that until we reached the merger at the end of the bridge and came to a grinding halt.

It was the first time we stopped.

No one made much of it until we didn't move. The clock ticked away, the silence was thick on the bus. My heart raced out of control every time I looked at my watch.

I took it off and shoved it in my pocket. Looking at it wasn't making the bus go faster.

The bus driver stepped off the bus as we all watched, then he got back on and grabbed the radio. "This is seventeen," he called over the radio. "I thought they cleared the lane. Anyone know what's going on?"

There were a few blips of static, then finally a voice. "They had it cleared. Civilian traffic broke through and now it's all jammed up," the person said. "We're at a stand still on Bigalow."

Bigalow was the road that drove straight toward the city but was my like a bypass and looped around the edge of downtown.

My heart dropped to my stomach.
We weren't moving.
In fact, it didn't look like we ever would.
My God, despite all my efforts, crash course in survival, the packing, the planning … it didn't matter.
We were trapped.

EIGHT – STEEL BOX

"Has anyone heard anything?" I called out, looking around. My phone was buried in my bag and it was quicker to ask.

The moments that followed, after finding out we weren't going anywhere, were a soup of emotions and behaviors. Crying and panic, anger, a couple rushing to get off the bus.

The bus driver urged calm.

"Anyone?" I asked again. "I know it's close, has the news said anything?"

"I'm checking now," 2C said.

"Why bother," said the woman across the aisle. She had been quiet the entire time, alone on the bus. A woman in her mid to late fifties with shorter brown and gray hair. She looked tall, although it was hard to tell with her sitting down, but she was thin, a weird thin. As if she was heavy at one time.

I looked over to her and she kept biting on her bottom lip. Nibbling quickly and nervously.

"Excuse me?" I asked politely.

Her head moved a bit when she talked, again, a product of nerves and there must have been something about that bottom lip because when she spoke only her top lip was animated.

"Why bother," she repeated. "There's nowhere to go. Nowhere far enough to run to."

I turned around to 2C. "Anything?"

"I'm looking ..." his words trailed. "Now." Slowly he lifted his eyes to me and I watched his Adam's apple move up and down as he swallowed harshly, then dropped his voice to a whisper. "They are saying take cover. The police and military left their posts. No one's out there keeping order, that's why the lane is jammed."

I closed my eyes briefly. "Jesus."

"Mommy," Macy whimpered.

I grabbed my bags and held out my hand to her. "Come on,

we're going." I looked at the woman across from me and spoke gently. "Wil you come with us?"

"No, no." She shook her head. "I'll meet my maker here."

"That's ridiculous." I slipped into the aisle, pausing to let 2C get out. "You're coming, right?"

"Sure, why not." 2C said.

"Where are you going?" Another man on the bus asked. "There's nowhere to go. We're too close to the city."

"We're at the edge of the orange zone," I said. "I don't know if that will matter, but I have to believe it means some sort of hope." I moved forward.

"Yeah, well, be realistic. In this area there's only hope if you find a lead bunker underground." Pessimist man said.

I stopped.

"What?" 2C asked.

I knew he saw it. I felt my entire face change expression.

"What do you know?" He asked.

"Steel," I whispered and locked eye. "I know where to go."

2C inched back to let me through. "Lead the way," he said.

I started to, then when I got to the front of the bus, I saw 2C was talking to the woman

"Please come with us," he said. "Won't you? She said she knows where to go."

The woman looked at me, then 2C, she nodded and stood.

Both of them headed my way. Pessimist man was behind them. I didn't know if he was following or going his own way.

It didn't matter.

Just as we reached the front, the bus driver said, "Sit back down, looks like we're moving."

The bus jolted slightly as he took it out of the parked gear.

"We're moving," Lip woman said. "Should we sit down?"

I looked down at my bare wrist then to 2C. "Should we sit?"

He shook his head and leaned to me speaking softly in my ear. "There's no time."

Hearing him say that made my stomach thump and I hurried

to the door. "Let us out."

"I can't, we're moving, we ..."

I then blasted my loudest, almost maniacal voice. "Let us out. Now. Now! Now."

"Fine!" The bus driver yelled, and the bus doors opened.

People on the bus were screaming for us to hurry.

No worries there, I high tailed it off the bus and on the bridge.

2C, the woman and pessimist man exited the bus and it rolled at its snail's pace.

"Traffic is moving," the woman said. "Did we do the right thing? I listened to you," she said to 2C. "Was it the right thing?"

"Trust me. It was." He looked at me. "How far is it?"

"Not far at all. How much time do we have?"

"Not much," he answered.

"I need to know how much is not much. Do we run, walk, what?" I asked.

"Bombs will come about fifteen minutes to half an hour after times up."

"Okay," I said. "So, when is time up?"

"We have nine minutes."

Instead of panicking or freaking out, I held onto my daughter and moved onward at a steady but quick pace.

I always imagined on true onset of war, or if there ever were bombs coming we'd hear the sirens of the civil defense blaring all over.

There were none. Anyone who could have rang the Lamar's had long gone and left post. In fact, there were no sounds. No screaming or sirens.

Everyone had left, taken cover or were sitting on buses stuck on the bridge holding out hope they were getting out.

I spotted a sole person running here and there. That was it.

We made it off the bridge and through the intersection that led to the barricade of Liberty avenue.

"When we get inside," I stopped to tell the three of them. "Grab water from the kitchen. We have bottles. You ..." I looked at the woman.

"Joan," she said. "My name is Joan."

"Joan, can you just start grabbing tablecloths. We need those. Just grab them."

"Yes. Yes. Absolutely."

"Where are we going?" 2C asked.

"About two blocks past the barricade," I replied as I started to walk again. "To my work."

"Mom, are we gonna be chased by zombies?" Macy asked.

It was an off the wall question, considering I had been honest with my daughter. Wanting to get moving and not get into any explanation, I muttered a, "No. No, we aren't."

She grunted a 'hmm' and I noticed she wasn't moving. I peered down to her and saw her focus elsewhere. I shifted my gaze to the direction of her stare and saw the police car twenty feet away. The driver's side door was wide open, but the rear window behind it was smeared with blood.

"Are we going?" 2C asked. "We need to go."

After telling Macy to stay put I walked over to the squad car. When I neared it, I saw a forehead resting against the window. There was a person in there, and I inched even closer. The face was hard to make out, it was streaked with blood. The second I got a good look, his eyes popped open, causing me to jump back.

Before I could scream or react, he mouthed the words, "Help me."

"Oh my God. Someone give me a hand." I reached for the door handle as Joan made her way to help.

She forced a nervous, closed mouth smile locking eyes with me as I opened the squad car door.

When I did, as I suspected, the young man rolled out,

catching his balance somewhat before completely landing on the concrete.

Both Joan and I reached down to him.

He looked up at me. "Thank you." His voice was hoarse.

I froze when I looked at his face.

"Do you know him?" Joan asked,

I felt a slight ache for this young man. He was someone's son, someone out there was worried about him and he was forgotten and abandoned in the back of a police car. The bloody forehead had to be from his constant attempts to do whatever he could to get help. Even if it meant banging his head against the window.

"I don't know him, but I recognize him," I said. "This poor kid was arrested yesterday morning."

Almost in shock, Joan asked. "He's been in there this whole time?"

"Can we go!" Pessimist man shouted. "The nine minutes has come and gone. We're on borrowed time."

"What about the handcuffs?" Joan asked.

"We'll figure out something," I said. "We don't have time right now. Can you walk?" I asked him.

"Lead the way," he replied.

"We'll get you cleaned up when we get there," I assured him, he took my daughter's hand, moved hurriedly down Liberty to the Peaceful, Easy, Feedary.

I kept looking back. Joan didn't leave his side.

No more was said the rest of the hastened journey. The keys to the restaurant where in my backpack, and I opened the front door.

It hadn't been looted nor the windows busted like a lot of other shops.

Once inside I repeated my directions of grabbing water.

But told them all to hold off on the tablecloths as I went behind the hostess counter and grabbed a box.

"Where are we going in here?" 2C asked.

"To the basement," I answered. "There's a huge walk in cooler. Interior safety, so we don't get stuck. There's a walk in freezer down there too, not as big. We'll need the tablecloths for warmth."

"Until the power goes out."

I looked inside the box to the remaining small, oil table lamps. "Joan, help me gather the little lights before we whip off the tablecloths."

"You're very smart, you're thinking ahead," Joan said.

"I'm not that smart, trust me."

"What about me?" the young man asked. "I can't do much."

"Yeah, you can," I told him. "Get my daughter to the basement. The doors in the kitchen. We'll be right there."

He agreed and walked to the back with Macy.

It was a lot of rushing, pessimist man taking cases of water downstairs while Joan and I gathered up the tablecloths and whatever else we could think of.

I tossed my duffle down the stairs so my arms could be free.

I wasn't sure what 2C was doing, he was rummaging around the kitchen and his arms were full when he stepped into the dining room, announcing. "Times up."

We had cut it close.

So far nothing had happened, and I still held on to hope that it wouldn't.

Once downstairs and securely in the fridge. 2C dumped the lettuce bin and I heard the pulling of tin foil.

"Everyone shut off your phones and give them to me," he said. "Hurry."

I had to reach in my backpack for mine. It was already off, I handed him it and the power packs. "What are you doing?"

"Making a faraday cage." 2C shrugged. "Not sure if it will work, but it's worth trying."

I paced back and forth looking up to the ceiling as he buried the electronics in foil, then covered the bin.

"Will this hold? Will this work?" Joan asked. "What do you

think?"

She was asking me. "I know they reinforced the floors three years ago."

"This is insulated," pessimist man said. "Cased in steel. As long as it's not a direct hit. We ... we may have a shot at this. Good thinking," he told me. "Thank you."

"Don't thank me yet."

I looked at my daughter who sat on a produce crate, a black tablecloth draped across her shoulders. I walked over to her and sat down near her, taking her in my arms.

"Maybe it won't happen," Joan whispered. "Maybe we'll get lucky."

We sat there in a fear filled silence, waiting, saying nothing. It wasn't long before we had an answer and we knew Joan's words were mere wishful thinking.

Reality struck.

The interior light in the cooler went out.

It was happening.

NINE – BREATHE

I didn't believe any of us knew exactly what to expect. I know I didn't. It was completely dark inside that cooler. I could see in front of me, and the only sense I tapped into was the feeling of holding onto my daughter in the moments before it started. Once it did, once we were positive the bombs were falling, I felt like I had been swallowed into some sort of black abyss of terror. Unable to see, only hear and not knowing what it would bring was frightening. Were we close or far enough away? It started as a slight rumbling beneath our feet. It grew louder and louder until we heard the bangs and crashes and the roar of what sounded like a freight train rolling right over our heads. Just as it started to calm it rolled right back again. What was happening? Was it one bomb, two? I just didn't know.

It sounded and felt like the entire world collapsed above our heads. Things rattled off the shelves and things banged against the cooler.

With walls of the unit so thick with insulation and steel, and noise too loud, it was conceivable that it could collapse like a house of cards at any moment.

Once it was quiet, once I felt confident enough to exhale, holding my daughter and breathing out in relief that we were fine and made it, 2C lit a flashlight.

"Is everyone okay?" 2C asked.

I nodded, but I don't think he saw it. "There's a flashlight somewhere in here, a bigger one. One in the freezer as well."

"I'll look for it," 2C said.

Joan blurted out a, "No. Not yet," and she fumbled with the box. "You might want to save that flashlight for another time. Okay?"

A few sounds of a flicking lighter and she lit the first of a little table lantern.

She grabbed another and lit that. Placing it on the other side of the cooler.

My daughter groaned a tearful. "Mom, I'm scared." Then wedged against me.

"So am I." I pulled her closer if that was possible.

Holding her tight I looked over to notice that the lanterns gave the room a soft glow.

Pessimist man grabbed his backpack, digging into it. Strangely enough he pulled out a notebook and pen, then looked at Joan, "Could I have one of those lanterns? I won't be that long".

Joan handed him one, lighting it. And then she proceeded, oddly, to start picking up the heads of lettuce that 2C had dumped on the floor. Probably to make room.

The young man with the handcuffs had scooted to a corner, his bloody face looked terrified.

I was in shock and unable to move, yet Pessimist man wrote fervently in his notebook.

"What are you doing? I asked.

"I'm working on how long we can safely be in this room and breathe."

"You mean before the air runs out?"

"Running out of oxygen isn't the concern" he said. "That's not our worry. It's how long before the air turns deadly. And even before that, we could be useless."

"Are you a scientist?" I asked.

"More like a farmer," Pessimist man said, "We breathe in the air, but every time we exhale, we exhale about 5% CO_2. That builds up. Each time we exhale we disrupt the balance of oxygen and CO_2. The higher the CO_2, the more deadly. We're all stressed, whether we like it or not, we'll breathe faster, producing more CO_2. We're in here, we're going to feel tired, that's not boredom, it's CO_2."

I asked how long.

"Ten percent level is deadly, so I'm assuming three percent CO_2 is the highest level we can go to be safe." He scribbled.

"This room is maybe twelve by twelve, eight feet high. That's 1152 cubic feet. We as humans, exhale one point seven cubic feet each per hour." He held up his finger. "That's high ended. That's talking, breathing heavy, worrying. Now going by the cubic feet of this room, that is thirty-four point five hours before we reach three percent. Take each person in this room, we'll say four point five," He pointed to Macy then wrote down, "And multiply that by one point seven, the amount of CO_2 we produce per foot. That means we're producing seven point six-five cubic feet of CO_2 per hour, divide the hours in this room by that, you get ..."

"Four and a half hours," Joan spoke softly. "Before we hit three percent."

He looked at her. "Did you just figure that out off the top of your head?"

"I'm a ... I have a knack for math," she said nervously. "Always have. Doing that same math, it's ..." she paused. "Fifteen hours before the room hits that level."

He wrote down to check and looked up surprised. "You're right."

"I hate math," said 2C.

"So, what do we do?" I asked.

"We have no choice," he answered. "Every three or four hours ..." He looked at the entrance of the freezer. "We open that door."

TEN – FAMILIAR

What was out there?

I asked 2C to borrow his flashlight and I examined the ceiling of the cooler. Was it dented or warped, was the entire restaurant sitting above us and any single movement above would crush us?

Not that I would know what to look at, but surely, I'd see something that would indicate the roof of the cooler was bearing tremendous weight.

We were all pretty reasonable, level-headed and strong in those after moments. I supposed that all would change as the clock ticked by. We were all in shock, plus we only heard the noise, we didn't see what happened.

It wasn't real yet.

We didn't know what lay outside that door. What would happen when we opened it? Would the basement be nothing but an open pit? The building above us completely gone. In an attempt to grab fresh air, would we also let in a ton of radiation?

That's if we would even be able to open the door at all.

There was a distinct possibility that the door wouldn't budge, then again, letting in oxygen wouldn't matter. We'd all pass out and die.

I didn't think much about what would happen after. Where we'd go, what we'd do, that was all a discussion we would have after we figured out if we could actually get out of not only the cooler, but the basement as well.

In three or four hours we would know.

I tried to focus on other things. Joan was helping the young man into bringing his cuffed arms to his front. It wasn't easy, it took some maneuvering. He groaned a lot in pain. His wrists, arms and shoulders had to have been hurting. Finally, he did it, breathing heavily after he did. Macy whispered she felt bad for the boy. If my nine year old daughter referred to him as a boy, then he was young. I grabbed a bottle of water, opened my duffel bag and pulled out a roll of paper towels I had shoved in there.

"Hey," I said softly to him. "It's not much, but can I clean you up?"

He nodded.

I poured some water on a towel. "What's your name?"

"Kevin,"

"Kevin, I'm Henley, but call me Henny." I started to clear the blood from his face, then noticed the gash. "I'll bandage this as soon as we clean it."

"Thank you."

"I take it this happened when you banged your head against the window?"

"No one heard me," he said. "I tried everything. They forgot about me. People just walked by. Could I ... could I have a drink of that? I haven't had water in a day."

"Absolutely," I handed him the bottle and fetched another.

When I retrieved it, Pessimist Man looked at me.

"Shouldn't we conserve?" he asked. "I mean ... we're limited."

"I know. But his wounds need cleaned. I'll go without if need be." I returned to Kevin. "I know it's cold in here. Probably won't be for long." I continued to clean his forehead gash. It was hard to tell the color of his hair, the front was a tangled mess with blood. "Tell you what, if we open that door, and the basement is intact, there's a freezer down here. I'll get you some ice."

"Thank you for being nice."

"How old are you?"

"Twenty."

"What did you do?" 2C asked. "I mean, why did they arrest you?"

"I was trying to get to my mom. I just needed to get to my mom. She works at the hospital. It wasn't my car, it was my friends and they shot the tires out. Then they said I stole the car. I kinda freaked out. I was mad, you know, then they arrested me." He reached up with his cuffed hands and stopped me., "Thank you. I thought I was going to die in that police car."

2C walked over. "You should have. It's a miracle you survived at all. We'll figure out a way to get those cuffs off of you. Just …" he reached down and examined Kevin's wrists, they were bruised and cut. "Try to be careful." He took the water from my hand and gently poured some on his wrists. "I'm Mark, by the way."

His name was news to me, I never bothered to ask him, I would have eventually. A few moments later, Pessimist Man let us know his name was Ted.

We were all strangers together in this situation. While I was certain we'd get to know each other, we started talking. Talking kept us calm.

Ted did convey that talking sped up the CO_2 process.

It didn't matter, we'd have to open the door anyhow.

Listening to them talk, kept my mind off the anxiety of unlocking the cooler.

Ted was a middle-aged horticulturist at the conservatory. Unmarried, no kids. He was talking to the kids at the Charter School when things fell apart. He tried to get out of the city to his home twenty miles south, but when he left the school, he learned his car had been stolen.

Kevin felt the need to interject and say, "It wasn't me."

Ted smiled at that, then told us he tried to make it home, called for rides, waited on buses, but to no avail, he was stuck. He had a ride out with a teacher, but like us, was stuck in traffic and opted to head back to the evacuation buses.

Mark told us he moved to Pittsburgh from Florida. "Personal reasons," he said. "But the job was here. I was staying a hotel until my apartment was ready. It wasn't my first choice, but the area was cool."

"What was the job?" Ted asked.

"Security systems at the county jail. I ran the computers, monitors and stuff." He shrugged.

"A computer guy," Ted said. "What are your thoughts about this virus that started this mess?"

Mark shook his head. "I'm baffled. Computer viruses are so common, but to infect these systems, this was a widespread operation with inside people. Homegrown terrorists."

"No kidding." I cringed after the sarcastic comment slipped out. "No offense to your computer skills. That's just … I'm sorry. That was rude."

"It's fine," Mark replied. "Doing computers is still fairly new to me. I was a cop in Florida for a long time."

"A cop," I said. "Well, then you should be able to figure out how to get him out of those cuffs."

"I'm gonna try."

"Thanks. I'm not a criminal," Kevin said. "I went to Pitt Tech. Or did. Then I switched to CCAC. I was gonna be an architect. I had like six weeks to go until my internship. How about you?" he looked at Joan. "Bet you're a teacher."

"Me? No. No-no." she shook her head. "I am a receptionist for the Family Counseling and Crisis center." She shrugged a fake chuckle. "Which is funny because I don't handle crisis well, as you could see on that bus. Now … now all I keep thinking is about those poor people on the bridge. Still in their cars. The ones that never got out."

Her words instantly took us all back into reality and there was an immediate return to a somber feeling.

It wasn't a casual meet and greet. We weren't trapped in an elevator. Everything above had just been bombed. When that door opened, the world was going to be different and it wasn't long before we'd be face to face with the truth of all that occurred.

ELEVEN - BEYOND PLAIN SIGHT

I didn't complain about the cold because I knew it wouldn't be cold for long. With tablecloths draped over us like blankets sitting in a cooler lit by only three table lanterns, we grew more and more silent by the minute.

Occasionally we'd talk about what we knew and what we learned from the 'how to survive a nuclear war' crash course the news threw at us.

None of us were really experts. Mark was the closest having had terror attack drills.

I envied the innocence of my daughter. She was scared but didn't show it. She didn't worry like the rest of us. I guess in her mind she was safe and with me, and that was all that mattered.

Macy showed confidence in my ability to protect her. It was a tall order to live up to, especially under the circumstances.

Not long before it was time to open the door, Joan began to get fussy and antsy. She insisted it was time and that she could feel the carbon monoxide poisoning entering her lungs.

Ted told her, "They call it the silent killer for a reason."

"I just know it's time. No one even has a watch. It has to be time," she insisted.

"I do," Macy said.

"Sweetie," Joan switched her demeanor to a pleasant one. "You are so nice, but honey, none of our watches work."

"Mine does. It's a wind up." She held her wrist to Joan's eye level. "See. It's six-twenty-five."

"Aha!" Joan snapped. "Thank you. It's time. Four hours. No wonder I'm suffocating."

"Jesus Christ." Ted walked to the door. "Okay. We'll do this. Move Macy to the back and behind the boxes as best as you can. Henny, you go, Joan you, too."

"Why?" Joan asked. "Because we're women?"

"Um, yeah," Ted answered. "Go back there in case there is

an inferno outside this door. Civilization may be dead, but chivalry is not."

I waited for Joan to ask him if the feminist movement had taken a cut as well. She didn't, she moved behind the back shelf with me and Macy.

We decided that Macy should be as far away from the door as possible, though I didn't know how twelve feet would make a difference if a blast of radiation came in.

I did however, doubt there was an inferno. Surely, we would have felt it.

Whatever was outside the door scared me, but it wasn't in the form of radiation or fire, but rather in our inability to ever get out of the basement.

That fear was reiterated when Ted pulled down the handle and pushed the door.

It stopped.

"Something is blocking it," Ted said. He put his shoulder to the door and pushed. "Not budging."

"Do we need to open it more than that?" I asked.

"Not for air, but eventually to get out," Ted answered.

Mark asked. "Can we worry about that later."

Ted shook his head. "Are you wanting to take a chance of something else falling and adding to it? I don't. We have to try to clear the door now before something accidentally makes it worse."

Mark joined Ted in pushing. It budged an inch, but not much more. Kevin helped, but they made very little progress.

Mark sighed out in frustration. "Someone has to go out there and clear it. And well, see what we are facing in the basement."

Joan stood up without hesitation. "I'll go."

Ted shook his head. "We can't let you do that."

"Why?" She asked. "I can fit through there and I'm strong. I'm very strong."

"I realize that." Ted said. "But ..."

"But nothing. I'm going. No arguments." She held out her

hand to Mark. "Can I have your flashlight?"

Mark handed it over.

"Thank you." She walked to the door and turned sideways to slip though.

"Are you sure?" Mark asked.

"Yes. Positive." She took a deep breath. "I have to pee." With only a little difficulty she squeezed out.

I envied her bravery, motivated by bodily functions or not. It took a lot of courage to be the first one to step out.

Now it was a matter of just waiting to find out what was really outside there.

<><><><>

It wasn't long, a few seconds maybe and Joan said," Ok, I see what it is. Looks like some sort of beam. I won't be able to move this by myself."

"Did it come from the ceiling?" Mark asked.

"I don't know. Yeah, it looks like a horizontal beam. I'm looking. The ceiling looks good, I think. I don't know."

"If the floor didn't collapse, it won't," I said. "The owners spent a fortune reinforcing the floor and ceiling, it could be one of the left over old beams. They had them stacked in the basement."

Joan continued to describe what she experienced. "It's not smoky, but it smells burnt. Like rubber. Looks like a shelf fell into the cooler. That probably was what banged. There are a lot of spilled large cans."

Ted looked at me with questions as he stood right by the door. "Were there a lot of cans down here?"

"Yeah, the bulky ones," I replied.

"There's a freezer. The door is still shut. Should I go in and see what's in there?"

"Not yet," Ted answered. "One of us will go with you when

we come out to move that beam. Just find a place to do your business."

"Thank you. I will," she replied.

"Tell her there's a small bathroom. Not much. More an enclosed Pittsburgh toilet."

Ted nodded. "Joan, there's a Pittsburgh toilet out there they made into a stall. Henny said use that."

"Tell her it's not very clean," I said.

Ted opened his mouth to repeat what I said then crinkled his brow at me. "Why does that matter?"

I shrugged.

"Okay, I see it. It's over by the stairs," Joan said. "It's so dark down here, I have to shine the light on the floor, so I don't … oh. Can you use a small meat cleaver to get those handcuffs off of Kevin?"

Kevin's eyes widened in terror. "No. No meat cleaver."

"Yes," Mark said. "I'll make it work."

"Dude," Kevin said. "You can't use a meat cleaver near my hands."

"Sure, I can," Mark said. "Joan let us know when you're done so we can come out and move the beam."

A minute or so later, I guess Joan found her relief spot, the cleaver slid in through the slightly opened door, then Joan followed. She handed the flashlight to Mark. "I'll let you two move that beam."

Both of the men went out. Kevin kept sheepishly looking at the cleaver. Macy asking me if they were gonna cut his hands off didn't help.

Mark and Ted fumbling outside the door, their voices were low and it was hard to make out what they said.

I focused on what was going on inside the cooler.

"What was it like?" I asked Joan.

"Dark. Very dark. We need to figure out a way to light it if we're gonna go out there."

"We can take the oil from the little lanterns," Kevin said.

"Make one big one."

"That won't last," I said. "None of these lanterns are going to last if we don't ration the lights. You'll have to use your math skills to figure out a schedule."

"We can't be down here that long, can we?" she asked. "I mean the bomb went off. That means all bombs, there are no more. It has to be safe to leave."

"There's radiation we have to worry about," I told her. "Plus, where are we going to go?"

"How long for the radiation?"

"I don't know," I replied. "I wrote things down in a notebook. I'll look. We've only been here a couple hours. I know it's not safe. Not right now. I remember the one guy saying the first eight hours are the highest levels. Or seven, I don't know."

"I wanna go home, Mommy," Macy leaned against me.

"I know, baby, but I don't know if we have a home to go to anymore." I pulled her closer.

"You know," Kevin said. "They had warning, right? What if they were setting up camps. Like help stations. Maybe once we get out …"

We all looked to the door when we heard Mark loudly whisper, "Shit."

Something about it cut through and we all looked at the door. A 'thud' preceded, both Mark and Ted rushing into the cooler.

I stood up. "What's wrong?"

"We have a problem," Mark said.

"What? What is it?" I asked.

"We're not alone." He pointed to the ceiling. "People are upstairs."

TWELVE – HUMANITY OR SAFETY

My first instinct wasn't to slam and lock the door. I didn't go into survival mode, fight for what we had, I wasn't thinking like that. "We have to let them down here."

"We don't know how many there are," said Ted.

"Well, how do you know they're up there?" Joan asked.

"We heard someone crying," Ted answered.

"Oh my God." I walked to the door. "We have to ..."

"Stop." Mark held out his hand. "This may be your place of business, but we ... we're all down here together. This should be a group decision."

"Did it sound like a lot of people?" Joan asked.

Ted shrugged. "I don't know. And can we keep our voices down. They'll hear."

"I'm sure they heard you two out there," I said. "They had to."

"Why didn't they come down here?" asked Kevin. "I mean that would have been the logical thing to do. Anyone who hears about bombs thinks, go to a basement."

"They probably tried," I said. "But I locked the door."

"Well." Mark said. "Obviously you worried about someone dangerous coming down if you thought to lock the door in the middle of everything. So if you thought about danger then, think about danger now." He leaned against the shelf and when he did, the clipboard we used to write down temperatures, fell to the floor.

"Shh," Ted blasted out.

"Oh, can I have that?" Joan asked. "I can keep track of rations."

Mark started handing it to her and stopped. "A paperclip."

"Yeah, we clip them together," I responded. "Every time we dropped that clipboard papers would fly. Why is that important?"

I watched him take the clip and hand the board to Joan, then put the clip in his mouth, biting on it.

"What are you doing?" I asked.

"Saving his hands. I could miss," Mark walked over to Kevin. "You know, if I use the cleaver. Can someone shine the light on these cuffs for me?"

Macy was holding the flashlight and inched her way over to them.

Mark crouched down. "Yeah, a cleaver wouldn't have worked. These are hinged cuffs. Not standard link." He lifted Kevin's hand and adjusted the light. "Hold still. No one make a sound." His hand maneuvered. There was a click. "That's what I needed to hear. The safety is on. One second …"

I heard the cuff release.

Kevin sighed out almost a laugh in relief. "Dude. Thanks."

Mark did the other cuff. "There."

"Thank you. Thank you so much."

"Now …" Mark stood. "We have another able body for protection."

"Are you that worried?" I asked.

"Yes," Ted answered quickly.

"Why?" I lifted up my hands then looked at Joan. "You're a crisis counselor. Should we be worried?"

"It's not been that long." Joan replied. "But the longer we leave them up there, the more desperate they'll become."

"We don't know how many are there," Ted said.

"Look, we're down here talking about this," Mark added. "How do we know they aren't talking about how to get down here?"

"I would," I said. "I would figure out how or at least try. You can't blame them for wanting to get to the safest place."

"Will they be okay up there?" Kevin asked.

"Absolutely," Ted shot out his answer.

"Not." I shook my head. "Absolutely not. These were nuclear bombs. There is radiation. I have a map I printed off the internet. It's gonna be bad. We may not even be safe, but we're a lot safer down here than up there. Every minute we leave them up there is another minute closer to death they get."

"What about food?" Ted asked. "Water."

"We have a freezer," Mark said. "We can use the melting ice from there and ration water. We have food. Again, we don't know how many people are up there."

"Mommy," Macy said softly. "I'll share my food. I don't want people to die because we're scared."

Ted pointed at Macy. "And that is what they're hoping. What's to say they don't come down here and force us out. Or worse."

"Right now, they're as scared as we are," Joan said. "Only they can see what is out there. We can't."

"We don't know that they're scared," Ted replied. "I don't mean to be a dick here. But they are not our responsibility. They aren't. What if they're sick, injured?"

"All the more reason to bring them down," I said.

"So, they what … get us sick?" Ted asked. "We try to help them. We're not doctors. What if one of them die? We'll get sick from that. Or, you know, what's to say they won't lock us in here until we suffocate?"

"Have you always been this paranoid?" I asked.

"I'm thinking ahead," Ted argued. "We can't just let a bunch of strangers down here."

"Four hours ago," Joan quipped. "That's what we were. Strangers."

"You guys stopped to help me," Kevin said. "I would be dead if you didn't."

Ted looked at Mark. "What do you think?"

"I think if we say nothing and leave them be," Mark responded. "They'll move on."

"And die," said Joan.

"Not our problem," Ted said.

"Look." I held up my hand, speaking calmly. "You said you

don't mean to be a dick. I'm gonna trust you aren't ... usually. And I am not trying to be a bleeding heart here. I'm not. Really, I am far from that. We may not be much safer down here, but we're safer than up there. Leaving them there, not offering them shelter, food, water ... help, that's wrong. It's only been four hours. Is this who we want to be? Selfish, scared ..."

"Alive," Ted interrupted.

"It doesn't matter. What good is being alive if we have to sacrifice people to do so," I said.

"It's survival, Henny," Mark said. "it's gonna be a different world now from here on in. There will be tough choices."

"Who says humanity needs to go down with the buildings," I told him. "If we leave them up there, exposed, to die, then we are no better than the people who did this to us. Now, I will stop arguing and debating and agree with what the majority says. But let's take a vote. What do we do?" I asked. "Bring them down or leave them to die?"

THIRTEEN – DECISION

It came as a surprise. Even with all the insistence that Joan made that the vote be anonymous, and the majority vote decided, even with her ripping tiny sheets of paper and sharing the pen, the vote was unanimous.

We'd bring them down.

I didn't get why we voted in the first place if everyone was going to vote like that. It was a waste of time. I guess talk is tough when discussing, but when push came to shove no one, not even Ted, could say, 'let them die.'

But one decision was not unanimous, it was who would go up and get them.

One person could go, but we thought it was best that two would venture up. One to stay mid-stairs in case of problems, and the other to knock and call out for them.

No one wanted to, but Mark volunteered and just as Kevin did, I stepped up.

It was my idea, my bleeding heart that pleaded their case, I would and should be the one to go.

After making sure Macy was safely tucked in the corner, I grabbed the flashlight that was stored in the cooler and joined Mark in leaving the safety of the refrigerator.

Upon first stepping out into the darkness, instantly my thoughts went to being exposed to radiation. Then I had to push myself to remember that we were in the deep side of the basement and on the other side of the wall was the loading dock lift that raised to street level. I was safe, at least down there from high levels of radiation.

I believed so, I didn't know for a fact. No one did. We weren't scientists or experts.

I had one advantage over everyone else. I knew that basement well. I knew how tidy it was kept to keep up with sanitation laws. That the only thing we could trip over was something that had fallen.

There was a strong odor of burning rubber, just as Joan described. I swing the flashlight beam from right to left trying to assess the situation.

Some boxes had toppled from the shelves, along with cans, but everything was miraculously alright.

I also lost the fear of being trapped down there. With the people upstairs that told me we'd get out. We may emerge into a dangerous world destroyed and different from what we knew, but we'd get out.

I could hear muffled cries above us, some shuffling, a cough or two. There were definitely people up there.

I couldn't make out what was being said, except one male voice sounding on the edge of irritation, "I know you're hurt, but there's nothing we can do. Please, please, please stop."

Mentally I couldn't chastise that man for lack of compassion because it was a stressful situation.

I couldn't imagine what they were going through, what they had seen.

I wondered if they found salvation in the kitchen. Maybe they shut the doors and were spared from too much exposure.

I led the way to the stairwell and allowed Mark to go first, I'd stay behind and waited half way up. I couldn't help but listen to what was going on above us. Mark was just about at the top and I had this thought causing me to whisper, "Wait, stop."

Mark looked over his shoulder at me. He mouthed the words, "Did you change your mind?"

I shook my head and waved him to come back down.

He looked irritated at me, but he backtracked.

"What?" He asked, whispering.

"We're not ready for them."

"What do you mean?"

"They're hurt. We're gonna bring them down here and offer them only protection."

"Okay."

"We should be able to help them."

"Jesus, Henny, none of us are doctors."

"I know, but you did hear Ted," I said. "If they have an infection or get one, so will we."

Mark ran his hand through his hair making it stand up even more. "What do you suggest?"

"I have the first aid kit in my bag, it probably doesn't have much," I whispered. 'But I'd say water and bandages. Maybe just get the water ready, rip up some tablecloths ..." I swung around the flashlight. "Here." I pointed to the box. "I don't know why I didn't think of this. New linens. New tablecloths."

"Henny," Mark said. "We don't have a lot of water as it is."

"Yeah, bottled water."

"Okay, what other kind is there?" Mark asked.

I shone the flashlight on the industrial plastic encased water heater. "This. 130 Gallons."

"Great thought but ... the water goes both ways. By now contaminated water has made its way into the lines and into the tank."

"Not if you shut off the intake valve."

"We didn't shut off the intake valve," he said with a shake of his head.

I only tilted my head.

"You shut off the intake valve?"

"It's really easy, it's just a valve handle. The gas, Paulo our maintenance man had the big wrench on the wall, and he made sure we knew how to shut it off."

"You shut off the water and gas?" Mark asked.

"I wouldn't have thought of that had WPXI not said if you have to retreat to the basement, secure it, and shut off the water and gas. They gave all those survival tips. I am sure a lot of people survived because of them."

Mark let out a sarcastic, "I'm sure."

"What was that about?"

"Why are we waiting to help these people? If you know we have water and new linen as you called it for bandages, what's the hold up?"

"I thought we'd get it ready."

"No, that's really stupid." He shook his head. "We don't even know what they need. Let's just find out then get things ready." He walked back to the stairs.

"Did you just call me stupid?"

A couple steps up, he stopped and turned to face me. "Really? Really? That's your main concern?" After another disgruntled shake of his head he made his way near the top, stopping just so he was close enough to knock.

I took my place halfway.

Mark raised his hand to knock. We weren't crossing that threshold into the upstairs, even though I couldn't figure out what made the big difference.

He didn't unlock the door, he knocked two times, and called out. "Hello. How many of you are there?"

There was no response at first, then the gut wrenching sound of a child's voice saying, "Daddy. There's a man calling out to us."

A child. While we were safe and cozy downstairs, there was a child up there. Maybe even more.

The sound of rustling footsteps carried our way above us and someone tried to open the door. They were unsuccessful.

"Are you gonna open the door?" The male voice asked. "We need to get below, I don't think it's safe up here. Can you open it?"

"Yes," Mark replied. "How many are you?"

The door rattled. "Open the door. You left us up here this long exposed. What the hell is the matter with you?"

"Hey!" Mark slammed his hand against the door to stop him "We had no idea until just now that you were here. I'll open the door. How many are there of you?"

"Six, Two kids. So, eight."

Mark looked at me, waved for me to back up. I did.

"I'm going to unlock the door.," Mark said. "When I do. Give me a second to back out of the way and then come down."

He slowly unlatched the bolt and hurried backward toward me.

They didn't wait at all to fling open the door.

It was bright, but not as bright as I expected. I ducked out of the way of the staircase and into more of the main area of the basement, watching from below as they began to emerge.

They couldn't see, it was far too dark for them.

The first one down was a man holding a young boy's arm, he wasn't carrying the child who looked to be about six or seven. The boy's eyes were closed, and his hands waved out as if feeling for something.

Was he not able to see?

"This way," the younger man said.

"Daddy, I'm scared," the boy replied.

Then I saw why the young father didn't carry his son, his arm looked mangled. Maybe it was the bloody and torn shirt, along with the dark that gave the illusion, but the father was injured.

He looked at me and said, 'Thank you.'

More people came down, slowly, all of them injured in some way. Two of them had to be aided. It was hard to see how badly they were hurt.

I looked for the other child, worried that they left him or her upstairs, until I saw it was a small infant, swaddled in a blanket in a woman's arms.

The final one, a man, maybe in his sixties closed the door behind him. He was the voice yelling at the other side of the door. I recognized it when he thanked us.

Including the children, there were nine in all.

They all stood there, clueless, as to what to do next. I was just as confused.

The only thing we could do was get organized with them

and see what we could do.
That was the best and only option at that moment.

FOURTEEN – ARRIVAL

I called them our kitchen survivors. Though I didn't know their stories at all when they first came down. Initially, it was calm, our kitchen survivors were a little shell shocked, maybe nervous. They crammed in one area of the basement until they figured out where to sit or what do to.

I still had my keys, which actually had a copy of the key to the freezer padlock, I locked it, even though we'd eat from there first, I still needed to keep track of things. That was Joan's suggestion.

Macy stayed in the cooler, the door not closed all the way. That was off limits. I wanted to help where I could, but I didn't want to leave her back there alone.

Ted offered to stay with her and alternate with Kevin. I was okay with that. After all, my first thought was how long really would these people need us.

It didn't take long for us to start situating. Moving people about.

We covered the concrete floor with tablecloths. Milk crates and vegetable crates served as chairs. We got them calm first, then figured out what we needed for them.

Joan ripped cloths for bandages, a continuous noise that seemed to never stop. Did we really need that many? I guess I really didn't look at them, not closely. Not at first.

"They're all hurt." His name was Van, an older gentleman, the one that yelled at the door. "One way or another. Some ..." he nodded, "More than others."

"What about you?" I asked him.

"A bump or scratch. Nothing major. Hell, I wouldn't even call it minor." He looked rough around the edges and sounded it, too.

"Keep them coming," a woman said to Joan. "Keep ripping. I need to keep them fresh," she then turned to Mark. "I need that water, one pan of water, nothing else, the other with soap, please, if you can find it."

She barked out instructions with authority. She had on a dirty green shirt from the restaurant, Samo's down the street. She wasn't old at all, maybe her late twenties at most. I figured she worked at Samo's and had some sort of medical training or was going to school for it. She presented herself that way. It made me feel good. We needed that. Maybe I was wrong. She brushed by Kevin making her way to Joan to get bandages. She lifted her eyes to me. "Will you be able to help me find things I need? I'm gonna have to make do with what I have."

"Absolutely," I said. "Can I do anything?"

"No," she replied. "Maybe after I get things situated. There wasn't much I could do upstairs at all. Here ... one at a time and then I'll let you know."

"So just stay out of your way?"

She nodded and moved away, first to the boy. He didn't look anywhere as bad as the others. Perhaps because he was a child, she chose to help him first.

"Adina," Van said. "Her name is Adina. She was a nurse at Children's hospital. One of the last to leave and got stuck there. I was taking people in my cab to evacuate, she got in."

"So, all these people were with you?"

"Good heavens, you think I can fit all these people in a cab?"

"I just ..."

"No." he shook his head. "Adina was. Mom and newborn were with me, another fella, never got his name and ... Whiney Wendy, not sure what her real name is."

I crinkled a brow wondering why he called her that until the young woman whined out. "Someone please stop that baby from crying. Please. My head."

"Get it?" Van asked. "No baby is crying. She hasn't stopped whining since before the bombs."

"Where did the others come from?"

"The boy and his father were already here when we arrived. This is one of the few still partially standing buildings. The kid looked at the flash, that's what Adina said. He can't see right now. The father, not sure what happened to his arm. We just got to this building not long ago. The others were on the street injured and they followed us."

"That's why we didn't hear you at first."

Van nodded.

"Where were you before this?"

"Samo's," He replied.

"Because she worked there?" I indicated to Adina.

"No, she didn't. She worked at Children's."

"I just assumed with the shirt and all ..."

Van shook his head. "She had to change it. There was some blood. You can say we cut it close. We cut it real close to the bombs. Traffic started moving, we almost got over the bridge. Then I figured if the bombs were coming, I wasn't making it unless I got cover. So, like everyone else, we ran. I knew Samo's had a basement and that's where we went. Headed straight there. Didn't really make it to the basement before the bombs went off. Made it inside, but not to the basement."

"Oh my God."

"It was scary."

Kevin stepped to us, "What was it like?"

"Kevin," I scolded motherly.

"What?" Kevin asked me.

"They just got here. It may be hard to talk about," I told him.

"Nah, it's fine," Van said. "I'm guessing you don't want to hear just that it was scary. To be honest. There wasn't time when it happened to be scared. We made it into Samo's just when the flash hit. It was like instinct to take cover. I hid behind the bar, crouched down as best as I could. The whole world shook. Things fell down all around us. I just did my best duck and cover."

"Loud," Wendy whiner spoke up. "It was so loud."

"The pressure, don't forget the pressure," Adina said. "One second it was rumbling, the next as the blast winds hit, all I felt was pressure like my head was going to explode."

"Until it reversed," the father of the little boy, Duncan spoke. His name was Tim. "It blasted one way and sucked back. When it did, it took every ounce of my breath away. I couldn't breathe."

Mark had been listening, he spoke up. "Was it a nuke? I mean, that sounds like a thermobaric bomb. Did anyone see the mushroom cloud, thermos wouldn't have a mushroom?"

Van shook his head. "I didn't see much."

"I did," the raspy voice spoke up.

I looked across the basement to the man who sat next to another person. I had yet to determine if that person was male or female. They huddled under a blanket, their face blackened with open red sores.

"I did," he said. "I resolved myself to die. I perched myself right at my window in this building to watch the world end. I knew not to look at the flash. That flash brought an eerie silence, then all hell broke loose. I saw it rolling in, not flames or fire, but debris, carrying like a tidal wave. I stopped looking and ducked down. I didn't expect to make it. I really didn't. Once it swept back out and I could breathe, I saw my apartment was destroyed and that was when I looked out."

"You saw it?" Mark asked. "You saw the mushroom cloud?"

"Two. They weren't next to each other and I could only see the tops, but I saw them," he answered.

The moment I heard that he saw two, I was instantly sick to my stomach. I excused myself and went to the cooler to check on Macy. I didn't need to hear the stories. I wasn't ready. Not yet.

"Take a break," I told Ted. "I'm back. You can go out there."

"I'd rather not," Ted replied.

"I don't blame you." I walked over to my daughter who was reading out of a book that seemed to big and too advanced for her. "Hey," I sat down next to her. "What are you reading?"

"Joan gave me this book. She had it in her purse. It's for a young adult. She's says I'm almost a young adult."

"That you are." I ran my hand through her hair. "Are you understanding it?"

"It's hard to see the words in the dark. It's making me tired."

"You sleep then if you want."

Macy nodded and closed the book, looking up to me. "Mom? What are they like?"

"The new people? Scared like us."

"Are they hurt?"

"Yeah, baby, some are hurt really bad."

"Do we know how to help them?"

"Not really. But ... the good thing is one of those people is a nurse. She's out there."

"So, she can help them all?" Macy asked.

"I don't know, Baby." That was the best answer I could give her. I pulled her closer hoping my embrace, having me there, would help her rest. "You know," I whispered. "You are so brave through this."

"No, I'm not. Not really. But what choice do I have right now?" She rested her head against me.

So smart, so mature, so right.

She didn't have a choice, none of us did. We could whine, cry, get angry, but it wouldn't change anything.

We were there. In that basement. The world as we knew it was gone and there was nothing we could do but sit there.

FIFTEEN – WARRIORS

The first four hours in the cooler after the bombs dragged by. It was us six, behind the safety of that door, counting down the minutes until we opened it to release the build up of CO_2. It didn't matter that we heard the rattling and banging or that we felt the vibration of the ground shaking out of control.

Somehow, it just wasn't real. I thought it would only become real once we emerged and went topside.

That wasn't the case.

It was real the moment those nine people came down into the basement.

They brought the reality with them.

I didn't know all their stories or whereabouts when the bombs hit, but they had to have been close, yet all of them had varied injuries.

Van, Adina and the mom with the baby seemed okay. Wendy Whiner or rather Beth, did have a head injury. Adina had said, if she could she would have sutured the wound. Beth also probably broke her collar bone. It was hard to tell. Adina assured us her pain was real.

As if we were the privileged ones, we stayed in the cooler, not that there was room for the others, but it seemed as if we marked our territory.

While the first four hours had dragged, the next eight to ten hours flew by.

We took turns helping Adina, refreshing the water, getting her bandages.

I grabbed one of the bulk cans of chicken noodle soup and was able to give everyone soup and crackers. It wasn't much. The next day we'd have a plan. Joan said she'd work on the food part, she wanted to so she could focus on something.

Sometime in there, we all dropped off falling asleep.

I dozed off, the day had caught up to me. I didn't dream of

the bombs, I dreamt about waiting to watch my favorite TV series. I woke with a crick in my neck from the way I sat with Macy. Carefully I slid her from me and rested her on the floor and I stood up.

It wasn't as quiet as I thought it would be. The sounds from outside the cooler had increased. Moans, whimpers and coughs.

"Can't sleep?" his whispering voice asked as Mark walked into the cooler.

"Actually, I did," I replied and stretched. "You?"

"No. I was helping out there." He pointed back. "Thought I'd get some sleep or try." He looked down to his watch.

"What time is it?" I asked.

"Three am," he answered. "Twelve hours. Twelve hours ago it all happened."

"It seems like longer."

"Unfortunately, yeah."

"Get some sleep. I'll go out and see if they need help."

Mark walked to the far side of the cooler.

"Hey," I called out to him. "How are they?"

He shook his head.

I didn't smell it when I was in the cooler, but the second I stepped out into the main basement area, the sour foul smell carried to me. It took me off guard for a moment. The basement was dimly lit with those little table lanterns. I saw Van and Adina sitting on the floor by the freezer across the room.

"Thought I'd offer my help," I said, approaching them.

"It's quiet now," Adina replied. "But soon it won't be."

"You should get some rest." I joined them on the floor.

"I keep telling her that," Van said.

"I'll rest soon. Some of these folks ... they just need care and compassion."

"I don't get it," I said. "I mean ... there was no fire, right? Why does Jeff have burns? He was looking out his window. And the other guy, he looks bad."

"He is bad," Adina said. "The boy Duncan, he has burns, too. They're flash burns. From the flash. Boris, the man you said is bad was on the bridge. I don't know how he managed to stumble back, but he did. Tim and his son helped him. His clothes are burned to his back."

I closed my eyes and cringed. "I didn't realize it was that bad."

"It's that bad," Adina replied.

"How did they know to come here?" I asked.

Van replied. "It was one of the few close buildings still mainly intact. There are others, yeah, but this was closest. They also said they saw us."

"We went down into Samo's basement," Adina explained. "But it was falling down on us, and we knew we had to leave. We covered up with moving blankets. Tim, Duncan and Boris were covered with beta particles when they came into this place. I had to do my best to clean them. We took clothes from employee lockers."

"I'm sorry," I said. "Beta particles?"

"When a radioactive weapon detonates on the ground it sends the debris up," Adina explained. "The debris comes down like snow and it is filled with radiation. Deadly ash snowflakes."

"They never mentioned that on the news," I said. "You know a lot."

"Not by choice," Adina replied. "It was part of a course we had to take at the hospital, especially when dealing with radiation, you learn a lot about it. I worked oncology at Children's."

"Oh my gosh, that is a hard job. I'm sorry."

"Don't be," she said. "I met wonderful people and saw a lot of miracles."

"You think we'll see a miracle here?" I asked.

"I think some …" She glanced over toward Boris. "Are too far gone for a miracle. Maybe for the rest of us there is hope."

"The rest of us?" I asked.

"We're close, Henny," Adina said. "To ground zero. Ground zero has the highest levels of radiation. Don't kid yourself into thinking there is none here. We may be sheltered from some, but not all. You can't smell it or see it, but it is cutting through us all. Some more than others. We may feel fine now, but in a few days, a week, we won't. It's hard to say. People react differently to radiation. The older you are, the less your body absorbs. In Hiroshima some wandered ground zero and never got sick, some were miles away and died. There's no telling what will happen, but make no mistake, the radiation threat is real."

The news was horrifying to me. I heard about radiation, but when she spoke of it, it was harsh. "Is there anything we can do?" I asked.

"Yeah, actually, there is medicine that counteracts it, blocks it. It helps flush it out of your system. It's out there. It's in the hospitals around here. In a day or two we're gonna need to make the hard choice to go get it. If we don't ..." Her head turned suddenly to the sound of violent regurgitation. She hurriedly stood up with an 'excuse me' and made her way to Boris.

I watched as she aided Boris who choked, coughed and vomited while she tried to give him comfort. She didn't finish the 'if we don't' part and I was glad she didn't.

"You okay?" Van asked.

"Yeah, I am. Wasn't expecting to hear that." My eyes strayed to the mother holding her baby. "That poor woman with the baby."

"Yeah," Van said. "A newborn. She said he was born a week ago."

I gasped. "She has to be so scared. She looks tired."

"Henny ..."

I slowly stood. "You know what. I may not be able to help medically, but I can help her."

"Henny, listen ..."

"No, it's okay. I'm just gonna give her a break." Without saying more, I walked over to the woman who sat nearer the stairs. I could see the baby was swaddled, not in a blanket but a tablecloth. She had one of those table lanterns on a box right by her head. Her eyes looked so big with the contrast of the light and her dirty face.

"Hey," I said crouching to her. "You look tired."

She only stared at me.

"Van said your son is a week old. I have to say, he is really good."

She closed her eyes briefly and nodded.

"If you want a break," I said. "I can hold him so you can sleep."

She slowly shook her head.

"Why not. I'll stay right here. Right next to you." I extended my arms. "At least move this little lamp so you can close your eyes and I can hold …"

My hand touched the lamp and that was when I saw.

The baby wasn't swaddled with a tablecloth, it only covered a knitted blanket that came over the boy's head.

The blanket was dark, almost crusted. But that wasn't what made me stop and freeze.

The child.

She held him close, almost hiding him, but I could see.

It was briefly, but it was long enough.

There was a reason I never heard the child cry. It wasn't because I didn't notice, it was because he never did. He never cried once.

The baby's eyes were partially open, as was his mouth, she had him curled into her chest and to the blood stained shirt she wore.

Even in the dark I could see there was no movement or life in that baby, and more crushing was not only the collapse of the left side of his face, but the deep indentation of the part of his head that pressed against his mother's breast.

Pressing my lips together, I set down the lantern. "I'll let you ... I'll let you be." I stammered the words, then I hurriedly stood and rushed away from her.

I don't know what I was thinking, but I ran to the rear of the basement and to the other room down there. The entire short run was riddled with the vision of that baby as my stomach churned and twisted.

No sooner had I made it to the loading elevator section, I heaved outward, vomiting what little contents remained in my stomach.

'Oh God, Oh God,' I thought, half bent over grabbing onto my knees, trying so hard not to throw up again. *That poor woman, that child.*

I breathed heavily seeing that baby was soul crushing, it was a shattering of any optimism I could have had.

"You alright?" Van asked as he joined me.

"Can I be alone?" I asked, staring down to my own puddle of regurgitation.

"She won't put the baby down."

My stomach wrenched and before I knew it ... splash! Another puddle formed at my feet out of my control, vomit blasted from my mouth.

"Can you blame her? She's destroyed," Van said. "I tried to stop you. To tell you. But you were already over there."

I took a few breaths. I still had that gagging feeling, my salivary glands were in full force, fighting the retching with an over production of saliva that poured from my mouth.

"When?" I asked. "When did he ..."

"When we were running." He paused. "She dropped him."

With another, "Oh God," I inched away, and my stomach twisted the last bit out as I held on to the wall for support.

"Adina couldn't save him. She tried. I'm sorry. We should have told you," Van said.

I wanted to scream. Just the thought of her running with that baby, so desperate to save him only to drop him was more than

I could handle.

"What are we gonna do?" I asked.

"I don't know," Van replied. "We don't have the heart to take him from her. Do you?"

I slowly turned around, running the back of my hand over my mouth. I slowly shook my head. I didn't. I didn't have it in me.

It wasn't something I wanted to think about any more. Not even a day had gone by and already without even leaving our sanctuary we were faced with the horrors of what had transpired.

If there was so much pain, suffering and heartbreak in the basement, I didn't want to think about what was above, let alone face it.

SIXTEEN – SLOW TICK TOCK

There was no day or night, there was only the hours that passed by. Some slower than the others, and each hour bringing something different.

One thing hadn't changed, Ezzie continued to hold her baby. The infant she bore a few weeks earlier was still cradled in her arms. I couldn't even imagine the horror of what she felt. Scared, young, wanting so much to protect her child but being the person responsible for his death. It had to be crushing.

She hadn't eaten or moved from her spot. She hadn't even gotten up to go to the bathroom.

I hadn't spoken to Joan yet about it, maybe she could talk to Ezzie. But to do what? We weren't going to be able to bury him. Were we to wrap him in a garbage bag and put him out like trash?

As tiny as his body was, in the twenty-four hours since the bombs, I could smell his decomposition. But that was the least of the smells.

It was horrendous and It was only one day.

Everything we smelled was related to sickness or injury. Smells, Adina said would eventually 'go away'.

Then Adina mentioned to me that she thought that room, the back room that led to the loading lift, or whatever you call those elevators that rise to street level, she thought it would work for the bodies.

Bodies.

Not one, not only the infant, but others. Who?

Boris was bad. That was a given.

In the twenty-four hours that followed he declined rapidly, spurting out occasionally with lucid moments about his time on the bridge.

We were closer than we hoped.

He insisted the fire hit the bridge. There were some arguments to that. One thing everyone could agree upon, Boris, Tim and his son, Duncan, had been exposed far too long.

Boris was already showing signs of sickness when he came into the basement, his vomiting and his hair was falling out in clumps. Tim and his son hadn't shown outward signs until the twenty-four hour mark. Then they started to get sick. It was mild, a headache, not wanting to eat. Fighting not to vomit. A fever.

Their wounds seemed to get worse overnight.

It was gut wrenching to think that another child was going to suffer.

And Jeff, the window guy. That small burn on the side of his face went from red to purple and glistened in the candlelight.

They were the first, they had been really exposed.

There were so many people in the basement, a part of me felt guilty for not wanting to give them names. When I did that, I made them real.

It wasn't at all what any movie depicted, or any experts told us to prepare for. I envisioned if I were in a shelter we'd be safe, fine, like we were in the early hours in that cooler.

Now, not only were we surrounded by the darkness of the basement, we were encased in the darkness the bombs had brought upon us.

And it was just the beginning. Only one day.

I wanted to run. I wanted to get my daughter and run. It wasn't safe, I knew the first chance I got, I was taking her and leaving.

Where we would go? I didn't know.

The time in the basement would be tedious, as if somehow that notion never crossed my mind.

It was far too early into the crisis for any person to have any job. Although, Joan seemed to always be counting and saying she was going to organize, and I would be the one getting the food. I think that had more to do with possessiveness over feeling like being the bomb shelter cook.

The restaurant was my place of employment and had been for a few years. Of course, I'd have a sense of entitlement. It was wrong, I know, but even after one day I started feeling like the host who just wanted her guests to leave.

They didn't mean to be intrusive or needy, but every time they took something to eat, every time they pissed in the wrong place, I got irritated.

It was wrong, no one in the basement deserved my feeling like that and I was careful not to act on it. Half the new people were sick.

Essie and the baby weighed heavily on my mind as well.

They were the main reason I did other things rather than being hands on with those who needed help.

Like water girl.

I emptied three more gallons into the bin and added the bleach to it like Adina suggested, then brought them to her.

"Thank you," Adina said. She looked exhausted, her eyes were half open, and I wasn't sure she even rested.

"Why don't you take a break?" I suggested.

"I will. As soon as I finish this round of wound control. I mean, if I don't do it, who will, right?"

"Someone might," I said.

"Maybe. It's not a pretty task." She sighed out a heavy breath. "I'll stop in a little bit. I do have a favor to ask you."

"What's that?'

"I know, and it's not to look a gift horse in the mouth, but is it possible, when you get the meal together it's something light or easy to eat. At least for half these people."

"Sure. We have cans of broth if —"

"Perfect," she cut me off.

"To be honest," I said. "We're limited to what's on the shelves and in the cooler right now. The stuff in the freezer is pretty frozen still and defrosting them with Sterno would take forever."

"Broth is great,"

"No one is really hungry," I said. "Maybe it's best for something light for everyone right now."

"Anything easy. Especially for the boy," she dropped her voice to a whisper, nodding her head to Duncan who sat next to his father. "He says his mouth hurts. Which means tomorrow it will be worse. I'm gonna go check on him."

My eyes stayed on Duncan, his head rested on his father's shoulder. His father seemed distant and in his own world, he didn't attempt to hold his son.

A large clank sound of something dropping caused both of us to jolt.

"Sorry!" Mark shouted out. "That was me. My bad."

"I'll go see what that was about." I said, then slipped away to where the sound came from.

It seemed like I moved from one section of a small space to another. Never really stopping. Not like Adina who constantly helped. I was more like trying to keep busy, to keep moving, looking for any excuse to not stop.

Stopping made me think, and I really wasn't ready to start thinking about everything we still had to face.

SEVENTEEN – WHO WE ARE

When the clunk of the dropping object occurred, it had an echo. It wasn't close, and that told me Mark was on the other side of the stairs.

The basement was set up like many basements in the city.

The stairs cut through the center creating two rooms. There was a third room, smaller, that was the one that had the lift that led to the street level of the alley behind the restaurant.

Everyone convened in the main room. It was bigger. The smaller walk in freezer and the large cooler. They stayed center, some chose to lean against the wall.

There was a shelf there with a few items, new linens, bowls, plates and more of those little lanterns.

Mark had dropped something on the other side of the staircase. It sounded like one of the large cans, probably soup or gravy.

When I went to the other side, he was standing by the open, cold cellar door. Like the Pittsburgh Toilet, those cold cellars were standard.

I was told, back in the day when the area was empty and the buildings were being constructed, they built the basements first, the workers or even families in some cases, lived in the basement until the upper levels were done.

We had come full circle back to living in the basement with nothing above us.

"Hey," I called out to Mark. "You okay?"

"Oh, yeah, hey. Found a ..." He held a can. "Gravy in with the non-edibles. Gonna move this on the other shelf."

"And try not to drop it?"

"Yeah," he nodded.

"Joan will be happy. It's another meal to mark down."

"Another meal," he repeated. "I just have the handy

clipboard and logging what we have in the non-edible. Never know what we'll need."

"That's a good idea."

"That is Joan's idea," Mark said. "She was really organizing that cooler. You know, the must eat now food and what can wait. I asked if she needed help and she said yes."

"So, she had you do this?"

"Better than sitting around."

"Or cleaning wounds."

Mark cringed. "Yeah, I'll pass. I'll do it if I have to. I prefer not to."

"I hear you."

"You know, if we were gonna have to wait it out anywhere, we couldn't have found a better place. We have everything we need here."

"I know."

"Might have to ration the sterno, though," Mark said.

"We didn't do a lot of private parties or catering."

"Doing this is actually a good thing. I can look for something in here maybe to mask the smell. I was thinking the laundry soap might help."

"It might. I doubt it. A lot of the smell is coming from the baby."

He produced a look of humored confusion. "I'm sorry, what? You mean his diaper?"

"No ... I ..." I paused. "You don't know."

"Know what?"

"How did you not know?" I asked.

"Know what?"

"The baby is dead."

CLUNK

The can dropped from his grip again.

"Sorry!" Mark called out. "My bad."

I bent down and lifted the can.

"Since when?" He asked.

"Since they got here," I replied. "It happened before. It was an accident."

"Oh, man." He closed his eyes. "Now I feel really bad saying something about the smell."

"It's okay. Adina wants to eventually get the baby, wrap him and place him in the other room. But whose gonna get that baby from her arms?"

"Joan." Mark answered without hesitation. "She's a crisis counselor, those people are good. Even if she hates being in a crisis. Look how she is down here. I'd get her on it."

"That had crossed my mind. I'll talk to her now." I started to step back. "Good luck with your task."

"Are there any other cleaning supplies down here?" Mark asked. "Besides the laundry stuff, drain cleaner and ..." he grabbed a can. "Bug spray. Which we don't need."

"You aren't gonna give that speech how cockroaches are the only guaranteed survivor of a nuclear war, are you?"

"No. why? Are they? Why would I say that?"

"Just heard that a lot on the news."

"No," Mark said. "I was just saying that because who cares about bugs."

"My daughter may disagree about the bugs. Speaking of which, I'm going to check on her and talk to Joan." Before he could stop me again, I headed to the cooler.

For some reason the first thought that entered my mind when I returned to the cooler was, so much for worrying about CO_2 killing us in there. The door was slightly ajar, which I believed was less for air and more so for the smell.

I stepped in and was surprised to see Van seated on a crate by Ted. Kevin was a foot or so away, back against the shelf, knees bent as he stared to his hands. His face had been cleaned up, and the wound on his forehead had butterfly sutures. Adina found time for him.

"Hope you don't mind," Van said. "Adina wanted me away from the sick."

"Everyone is not sick out there," I said. "At least I didn't think they were."

"She says they will be by tomorrow," Van said. "She doesn't think I will."

Ted asked. "How does she know without blood testing and such?"

Van showed him his arm. "My wound is healing. She said that's a sure fire way to know I wasn't exposed to much radiation. She explained that the body can't heal, and that's the first sign she looks for."

"Lucky you," Ted said.

"Really, are any of us lucky?" Van asked.

Kevin lifted his head. "I hope my mom was. You were driving a cab, how many nurses were left, do you know?"

"Not many," Van replied. "I only had one in my cab. And I know they were moving health care workers out first. Adina stayed behind to help. "

"Maybe she tried to reach you," I said. "You were in the police car."

"They had my phone, too," Kevin replied.

"See. Don't lose hope." I ran my hand over his head. "As a mom, trust me, she is worried about you. She tried to contact you. I believe it. She is thinking about you. More than likely, she'll be looking for you."

Kevin shrugged. "How will she even find me?"

"Eventually, people will have to emerge," Ted said. "And they had those evacuation centers set up. She'll probably look there for you."

Kevin seemed to halfheartedly accept that. I walked to the back of the cooler to check on my daughter.

She sat on the floor, Joan was behind her and oddly, was brushing her hair.

"Sorry," Joan said, pausing in the brushing. "I hope you don't mind."

"No, not at all. Macy?" I crouched down. "Is that okay?"

"It feels nice."

With a humming 'hmm', Joan continued to brush, long slow strokes against my daughter's brown hair. "I used to love brushing my daughter's hair. We'd brush it every night. I had to. I hated when my mom brushed my hair. Of course, she's all grown up now, married and living in Wyoming." She looked down to Macy and smiled. "Wyoming of all places."

"Bet she is safe," Macy said.

"I think she is." Joan winked. "I feel it."

"You have a daughter," I said. "I didn't know that."

Before Joan could say anything, Ted spoke up. "How much do we really know about each other? We've been down here a day and I don't know much about any of you. Two years ago, I was stuck on an elevator for three hours and there wasn't much I didn't know about the people in there with me by the time the doors opened."

"Stressful situations bring out different behaviors," Joan said. "You weren't faced with death. We're lucky none of us are angry ... yet." She paused then brushed again. "Maybe it is a good idea to know one another. I mean, it will help us understand reactions we may all have."

In the after moments of her saying that, there was silence.

A long silence.

Until Macy said, "This is awkward."

I smiled, nearly to the point of a laugh, "Why do you say that?"

"She invited everyone to talk and no one wants to," said Macy.

"I'm sure we all have time to learn about each other," I replied. "We'll get there."

I wanted to sit down, close my eyes for a moment. My post was in the far back corner. I had made a comfy pile of tablecloths for me and Macy and took my seat there. I could watch my daughter, and that was something I always enjoyed.

No sooner had I closed my eyes, I heard Kevin's voice.

"I don't like her," Kevin said,

"That's out of the blue," Van commented. "Who? Joan, Henny or the little girl."

"What?" Kevin blasted with a slight chuckle. "Not the little girl, that's so wrong. That girl out there. The one that's always whining and moaning. I don't like her and wish she wasn't here."

"Wendy Whiner," Van said. "Real name is Beth. Yeah, she's a doozy. She got in my cab and needed a way out. I was one of the last evacuation vehicles. But like I said that was out of the blue."

"Not really," Kevin said. "I just heard her whining again."

"Well, she is getting that sickness. Her cut on her face is spreading so it's probably painful. She at least has something to whine about."

"Serves her right," Kevin said.

"Whoa, wait." Ted spoke up. "Is this our mild manner criminal speaking?"

"Sorry, that's not what I meant. Maybe it is. I'm not a mean person. Honestly, I'm not, but Beth is heartless."

I had to ask. "Do you know her?"

Kevin shook his head. "I recognize the face. When I was in the back of the police car. It was way before you helped me out, she came to the car. She looked in the window. I screamed for help, begged her to help me, she started to, then ran away. I'll never forget that face."

Joan spoke up. "I'm sorry she did that to you. Stress does things to people."

"I disagree," Kevin said. "I say, like alcohol, stress shows you the real person. I mean, we're under this horrible situation, right? The world burned around us. Adina hasn't stopped. She is a good person. Joan is kind and worried. Everyone is showing a good human side. That to me tells me more about them than any story they can tell."

In his youthful wisdom Kevin made a lot of sense.

Unfortunately, I didn't agree.

All of us were being good, kind and patient, but we were still so early on, we were technically on our best behavior. We had lots of space, food and water, but as the days rolled on, and the walls closed in, I wonder how kind and patient most of us would be then.

EIGHTEEN - CHOICES

I had never seen anyone so desperate for a cup of coffee that they'd go through inventive leaps and bounds to make some.

Mark was that person.

Upon finding the box of coffee packets he was on a mission.

He managed it though. Using sterno, water, and a coffee filter, he brewed individual cups. I could smell the coffee, and it was a nice change of pace from the gag inducing odors.

Each cup took about three minutes.

It was worth it.

It was a bright spot to a new day that increasingly grew bleaker by the minute.

We weren't a hospital, but we were closed in a space filled with sick people.

Adina was still going, even though she told Joan she was starting to feel tired and a little ill.

I couldn't even walk into the main portion of the basement without wanting to scream. All I wanted to do was stay in that cooler and only leave when I had to.

Sadly, I had to.

Joan wanted me to come with her when she spoke to Ezzie.

Wendy Whiner increasingly complained that the smell of the baby was making her worse.

It got to the point where Kevin shouted out from the cooler. "Leave her alone. Shut up. Just shut up or go."

Forty-eight hours. The calm was leaving quickly and was replaced with tension.

It was to be expected.

Even though Wendy, AKA, Beth was loud, she was right.

The deceased baby was only adding to the unsanitary conditions of the basement.

"Will you, please, come with me?" Joan had asked.

I was sipping on my coffee, Macy sleeping across my lap.

"It's time that I talk to her, but she doesn't know me," Joan said. "You give her food."

"She doesn't take it."

"Still."

I nodded, set my cup on the shelf, then gently lifted Macy from my lap.

After being seated for a while, I had to stretch a little to work out the kinks. As I approached the door of the cooler, I could hear their voices, coughing, moans and a whimpering cry of a little boy.

"Daddy, it hurts," he said. "My mouth hurts."

"Try to have some water."

"I can't."

I had paused by the door, gaining the courage to step outside.

I knew it was going to be bad.

A mugginess had set into the basement making the smell seem thick, it stuck in my throat ready to choke me at any second.

"You ready?" Joan whispered.

I nodded.

"Take a breath," she instructed,

I did, but it didn't help.

So much had changed in the hours that I had stayed in the cooler.

There were less lanterns burning, and only a glow of a face here and there was seen.

How easily it was for me to forget the people that had joined us. I blocked them out, like a nightmare, but it all came crashing back when I stepped into the main room.

Adina was asleep in a chair, finally she rested.

Beth the whiner, paced in small circles, rubbing her arms and whimpering. Boris was finally resting. He had been so bad, in such pain that he'd randomly cry out, reaching for something that wasn't there, in almost a delusional state.

Tim had taken to holding his son, Duncan. I worried about that. He hadn't been cradling him and comforting him as he should have.

Jeff, the window guy curled into a ball holding onto a bucket as if it were a security blanket.

I followed Joan as she made her way over to Ezzie.

Joan gave me a nod, no words, I suppose I was to introduce them, and I did.

"Ezzie, this is Joan. She wants to talk to you," I said.

Joan crouched down by Ezzie, I waited to hear her talk her counselor speech. Something deep, something that would get through.

"Ezzie, Honey," Joan said. "You have to let us take the baby."

What?

All that and she was blunt and just blurted it out.

Ezzie just looked at her, shook her head once and whimpered out a, "no."

"Yes," Joan said. "I know this is painful. I know this is hard. But it isn't good for you or anyone down here to keep him in this room. He's gone, you know that, right?"

Ezzie nodded.

"We'll be gentle with him."

Ezzie nodded. "Can I … can I just hold him just a little bit more. Just a little. Then he can leave this room. Just a little."

"Just a little," Joan said. "I'll be back."

As Joan stood, Ezzie rolled the baby into her chest.

"Sometimes," Joan whispered to me. "You have to be direct."

It wasn't that easy. It couldn't be.

We left the main portion of the basement, returning to the cooler.

It was pretty early in the morning, at least I guessed it to be, and everyone was sleeping. Except Mark, he was hopped up on his caffeine.

I was glad to be back in the cooler. It was crowded and warm, but it didn't have a death trap feeling that the main portion of the basement had. Every time I stepped in there, I felt as if I were playing Russian roulette with germs.

I pushed the door to the cooler closed, not all the way, but enough to block everything out.

"How did it go?" Mark asked.

"I'm giving her an hour," Joan said. "Then we'll deal with it again. Sometimes it has to be baby steps."

Baby steps.

Did she just use that wording?

I felt so bad for Ezzie. A young mother not only consumed with grief, but her soul had to be swallowed by guilt.

We had been in the cooler maybe fifteen minutes, I had settled with Macy, finishing my cold coffee when Mark declared that he had forgotten.

"The lettuce bin, oh wow," he said almost randomly, then he pulled out the large bin, and lifted the lid. "Our phones."

The caffeine sent him into some sort of fast and furious mode. I hadn't a clue what he was talking about until he reached in the bin and pulled out a phone.

The phones.

We all placed our electronics into his homemade, rushed faraday box.

There was a sense of excitement quickly followed by a sense of disappointment because I knew, even if the phone powered up, who were we going to call. Would there even be a signal?

He passed out the phones to those who dropped them in the bin.

Admittedly, even I was excited to see my phone after two days. To power it up, but halfway through the cycle, Adina came into the cooler, putting a pause on our enthusiasm.

She leaned against the cooler door frame, like it was her

crutch. It was mainly open and I wished she would have left it like that.

A wave of smell carried in, but just as it did, I caught the scent of a new smell.

"Boris is dead," she announced.

There wasn't really any reaction to that. It wasn't a news flash, and we had all expected it. Me, I was stuck on the smell. It was a sulfur smell, not as rank as the others, it seemed to blanket the odors some.

"I am going to need help moving him out of the main portion of the basement, into the back room. I can't do it alone."

"I'll help," Kevin said.

"Thank you, and there is one other thing," her eyes shifted about. "I'm sick and I'm only gonna get worse. Everyone out there was exposed more than all of you. That's not to say you won't get sick. It won't be as bad. Remember I said there is a treatment. Before we end up with nine dead bodies, we need to try to help everyone."

"What are you saying?" Ted asked.

"Someone, more than one person, has to leave and get that help," she said.

Ted asked. "Like look for transportation or a medical camp?"

Adina shook her head. "Everything we need is two blocks away at the hospital."

"Is the hospital still standing?" I asked.

"I saw it. Yes, if not, Children's is."

"Wait. Wait." Mark waved his hands about. "Those people are sick with radiation sickness. There's' radiation out there."

"Boris, Jeff, Tim and his son ..." Adina said "Were exposed to fall out. Me and Beth, Ezzie, we left our shelter in the crucial hours where radiation was the highest. Radiation has a half life. If he waits until tomorrow and we go fast, it's low enough that risk is minimal. I can give a science lesson if ..."

"Hey where are you going?" Beth's voice carried to us from

outside the cooler.

It was evident, Adina was going to ignore her and keep talking, until the others were shouting.

"What are you doing?" Tim asked.

"You need to stop," said Jeff.

Adina spun and hurried from the cooler.

I followed along with Joan and Mark.

As soon as I stepped into the basement, I smelled the sulfur and rotten egg smell. It burned my nostrils.

"What's going on?" Adina asked.

I didn't need to hear the answer, I saw the empty space where Ezzie had been seated.

"She's leaving," Beth replied. "She's leaving."

Adina ran to the steps with me and Joan right on her heels.

"Ezzie stop," Adina called to her.

"Come back here, please," Joan pleaded.

Ezzie stopped and looked back at us. "I'm leaving. I'm not staying."

"Ezzie," Joan said. "I know this is hard for you. I know. Let us help you, please."

Ezzie shook her head. "If you want to help me, let me go. Just let me die. Let me die with my son. Please."

Joan and Adina pleaded. I didn't pay attention to who said what. I took a step forward, thinking maybe as a mother myself, I could help convince her not to leave, that was when my foot hit something. I felt it against the tip of my shoe and heard the soft thud and the sound of whatever it was sliding some on the concrete.

"Ezzie, please, don't do this."

"You need to come back ..."

It was dark, but I searched it out. What did I kick? When my hand touched it, I smelled the sulfur and I lifted it.

Drain cleaner. The bottle still had some in it, but it was no longer full.

"Don't go out there, Ezzie. Juist come back down."

"You're sick, we can help."

"Stop," I said softly. "Let her go."

Both Adina and Joan looked at me as if I were nuts.

I looked up the stairs. "Go on, Ezzie. Go on. Be at peace."

Ezzie gave a single nod, cradled the baby, took a few steps up, opened the door and left.

The door closed.

"Are you nuts?" Adina snapped at me. "You just encouraged her to go. She'll die out there!"

I held up the drain cleaner bottle. "She's already dead."

I turned from the stairs. Ezzie must have heard me and Mark talking, she sought out that drain cleaner. When she told Joan the baby would leave, she wasn't lying.

It was her way out. I didn't blame her. Not one bit. I wouldn't want to live either if something happened to Macy.

A part of me envied her.

It was over for Ezzie. The rest of us still had a long way to go. Sadly, at the rate we were going and what we faced, all roads led to the same place … death.

Ezzie was just getting there before the rest of us.

NINETEEN – BASIC MATH

"When?" I asked.

We had gone silent after Ezzie's departure, no one really wanted to talk or play with the recently remembered phones.

It wasn't what I signed up for.

Granted, no one signed up for an all out nuclear strike, but in my mind, my daughter's survival was forefront and all I cared about and wanted to care about. Now I was faced with emotions I didn't need or want.

Had I not let them into the basement, I wouldn't know Ezzie. I wouldn't know the tragedy of how she dropped her baby. I wouldn't know what fear smelled like and panic, or what radiation sickness looked like.

I probably eventually would.

If it was just me and Macy, it would be different.

Or just those of us who ran for the restaurant.

We brought the reality downstairs with us, I was the one who suggested it, championed for it, and now as we lived in it, those strangers became our problem as well.

"When?" Adina repeated my question. "As soon as we can. It's been two days. The longer we wait the safer it is up there, but the longer we wait the harder it will be to turn back some of the effects."

"There are other threats," Ted said, then paused to cough as if he choked on his words. "Up top. I mean."

"If people are up there," Adina said. "They are no threat."

"How do you know?" Ted asked.

"Because radiation kills. Up there they are fully exposed. You can get a lethal dose quickly, or slowly over time. The medication we need will stop our bodies from absorbing the radiation. One of them helps us eliminate it," Adina explained. "Our bodies can repair radiation damage, but not as fast as our bodies get damaged. Look at it like a slow running faucet going into a sink with a sluggish drain. Sure, some of the water goes down, but the sink will overflow eventually. The same applies for radiation."

"So, this medicine." Mark said. "Is like the drain cleaner."

Everyone at that moment, whooped out 'aw mans,' and 'come on.'

Mark looked clueless, "What? What are you ... oh, oh stop. That was not a dig on Ezzie, she ..." he pointed at Adina. "Brought up the clogged drain."

Van waved out his hands. "In any event, you're saying we need to go. Head to the hospital to get what we need for radiation sickness."

"Yes. But we need medication, we should get it. It's dark and damp, all of us are sniffling and coughing." Adina nodded. "The stuff for radiation is foremost. I'd say Children's, but it's too far and too big. You want to be out there for a minimal time. Radiation doses are measured by absorption per hour. Like I said before radiation has a half life. The more hours that pass the lower the radiation."

"So, like ..." Van said. "In a few hours, it is lower by half?'

"No," Adina shook her head. "It's tough to explain. It's a math thing. The best example I was given was there was roughly one thousand roentgens of radiation per hour in Hiroshima. After seven hours, that number dropped to three hundred, after another seven it dropped to ninety."

Joan spoke up. "So, it drops seventy percent every seven hours."

Adina shrugged. "This is what I learned."

Van asked. "How much radiation contamination is deadly?"

"It's all deadly," Adina replied.

"Oh, balls, come on," Van said. "You have to have an idea."

"They say the body can absorb up to one gray of radiation, or a hundred roentgens, before getting sick. Four or five grays are fatal. One or two roentgens per hour is safe for longer exposure."

"According to your percentages," Joan said. "If that seventy percent holds true, and it was like a thousand of those radiation things per hour, right now we are about eight or nine of those measurements per hour. So, it would be safe for us not to get sick if we were out like two hours."

"Depends," Adina answered. "We don't know how much we have been absorbing down here. Less for Macy because she rarely leaves this cooler. That doesn't mean she doesn't need the medication. She does. The sooner we get it to her, the lower her risk of getting sick. We'll know our levels down here if we get to the hospital, there are measurement tools.

"So right now," I said. "It's not a matter of when we can go or even if. It's who will go."

Adina nodded.

Optimally, it would be two teams for faster results, especially with two different areas of the hospital to hit.

Adina volunteered to go, but that wouldn't be wise. She was already sick, and the only medical person we had.

She said., "It's a given Macy can't go, and Kevin, you shouldn't go either. You're young. The younger you are the more your body absorbs, the older the more resistant."

"I'll go," Mark said. "I'm not quite old, but older than Kevin."

"Hell, if you need old," Van said. "I'll go."

"No," Adina replied. "You know what's up there. There's a lot of debris. Could be a lot of climbing and you have to move fast."

"You saying I'm slow?" Van asked.

"I ran to safety with you, remember."

Ted grunted. "What the hell. I'll go. I know the area. Make us a list."

"Then that's it," Mark said. "The two of us."

"No, no," Joan barked. "Don't be ridiculous. You need

more than just the two of you. The hospital may be a mess or even a waste and you may have to go to Children's. The more eyes, the better and faster. I'll go, too."

I really didn't give it any thought or debate in my mind, I just blurted out, "I'll go, too."

It wasn't that I wanted to go up there and leave my daughter. I had to. If Adina said Macy needed that medication as a precaution so she didn't get sick like Boris, then I was going to go. I vowed to keep my child safe, and the only way I would be a hundred percent sure we'd get that medication was if I went myself.

TWENTY – WAITING THE NIGHT

The biggest debate was a matter of when we would go. It was better for us if we waited, but worse for those who were already suffering.

Collectively we decided to wait until morning, or at least what we thought was morning.

As the day moved on and evening set in, I started to doubt that decision, even thinking we were selfish.

I had to keep reminding myself, I was doing this for my daughter and aside from preventive medication my daughter needed, she needed me, as well. If I got sick or even too sick to do anything, what good would I be for her?

Macy was my top priority.

But Duncan, the little boy, pulled at my heart strings.

Adina had said she didn't think Duncan and his father, Tim would be far behind Boris, only because they were all exposed at the same time and made it to the restaurant together. Boris had suffered burns.

Jeff wasn't far behind them, and Beth, along with Adina trailed the field.

Van had still not shown any symptoms, or at least hadn't owned up to it.

It had to be horrible to those knowing they were sick and watching the others, knowing that could be them.

Of course, they were all exposed to various levels of radiation, so it was hard to say if Beth and Adina would even get as bad as Boris ... or even Tim.

Just before Boris passed away, he groaned in his sleep. Often times, crying out, ejecting to a sitting position, grabbing for things that weren't there, scratching at his own skin, searching for his water, which was right there with in his reach. He suffered not only physically, but mentally.

Tim began to do the same thing. He sat up several times

looking for his keys, refusing to come back to any reality that he was in a dark basement.

He argued and fought.

Maybe that was for the best. Maybe he didn't feel sick while being stuck in his own delusional world.

Duncan however paid the price.

He couldn't see his father, having suffered from flash blindness, but he could hear his father's anguish and Duncan cried.

He cried so much.

His father didn't seem to notice.

I felt helpless as to what to do. I listened as I held my own daughter. I fell asleep for a little bit and woke up to Duncan screaming horribly.

Just as I started to go to him, I heard Joan's voice.

"It's okay, baby, it's okay." Joan spoke soothingly,

I lifted a little lantern to use as a light and made my way out of the cooler.

Joan had taken the little boy into her lap, holding him tightly with a tablecloth wrapped around him.

She looked up to me with such a lost and painful look in her eyes.

"He says his mouth hurts really bad," Joan said.

I stepped forward and brought the lantern closer to him. I thought for sure I wouldn't be able to see anything, but the open sores around his mouth were huge and glistening when the light hit him.

"He won't take any water," Joan told me.

I immediately turned and walked over to where Adina usually sat by the freezer.

At first, I didn't see her, then I noticed she was laying on the floor on her side.

I lowered down to the floor and gently touched her, whispering, "Adina."

Startled, she sat up. "What? What's going on?"

"Duncan is really in pain," I said. "His mouth is really hurting him. Is there anything we can …" My final word 'do' didn't come out of my mouth. Like with Duncan, the lantern, though dim, was bright to show me her eyes were glossy, and her face had developed a sore just left of her mouth.

"Okay, I'll see what I can do," Adina said.

"No, you know what? Lay back down," I instructed. "I have an idea."

"You sure?"

"Yeah, lay down."

She didn't say anything further, her head plopped back down. Sick or not, she had to be exhausted and it had to be catching up to her.

I wasn't lying to her, I did have an idea and the inspiration for it was literally right in front of me.

The walk in freezer.

Even though the power had been out for two and a half days, so much was still frozen. One of those things was the five gallons containers of chocolate ice cream.

I knew not only would it be cold, it probably was still pretty solid. Especially that chocolate.

I hated retrieving ice cream from those carboard cylinders. I hid the chocolate in the back and told customers we were out. The last time I tried to get ice cream from it, I got a blister.

When I found it, it was still pretty thick, I grabbed the whole thing carrying it from the freezer with me.

On the back shelf where the extra dishes and silverware were located there was a bin of those silver ice cream bowls, I grabbed one, a spoon and found serving utensils.

I scooped up a big old heaping bowl and for the first time in as long as I could remember it wasn't a tedious task.

Duncan sat up, his tears stopped when he saw the ice cream.

"This will cool your mouth," I told him. "Do you want to try?"

He nodded.

I placed some ice cream on the spoon and brought it to his mouth.

He was timid at first, wincing as he took it in, then he smiled.

"Think you can eat that?" I asked.

Duncan nodded.

"Here," Joan said. "Let me feed you."

I handed the bowl to Joan, then lingered like a bad odor until I realized I was just an observer serving no real purpose standing over them.

I was headed back to the cooler when I paused and went back to the chocolate ice cream.

Yes, it was three in the morning, but I got a little bowl for myself, Macy and Joan.

Joan smiled and thanked me, I set her dish on the floor next to her and took mine and Macy's back with me.

It didn't take much effort to wake my daughter or anyone else in the cooler. As soon as I told Macy, "Hey I got you chocolate ice cream. "It was like a loud alarm clock. Everyone woke up.

"Ice cream?" Kevin asked. "Who has ice cream?"

I told the others where I had left it and one by one, they went out to get some.

Macy smiled as she ate hers. She needed a treat, something good amongst all the bad.

The ice cream worked on Duncan as well.

Mark told me when he went to get ice cream Duncan looked happy sitting on Joan's lap, eating.

It made me happy that in some small way I had helped him.

The poor child who suffered in pain and sickness, found solace and relief in that ice cream.

It calmed him down. So much so he didn't cry or scream the rest of the night.

I was able to fall back to sleep in the silence.

It was only after I woke again Joan told me Duncan had

found another relief from the pain.

Not long after he finished his ice cream, Duncan passed away.

TWENTY-ONE – JOURNEY

The little boy deserved so much better than we gave him. He deserved some sort of a sendoff rather than being placed in the back room of the basement. There was nothing more we could do other than bow our heads in a silent prayer. What made it more sad than placing him there was the fact that his father never noticed he had passed away. Maybe that was a good thing. Duncan's father was not far behind him. I suspected no medication we got would help him. He was too far gone. It would, however, help Adina and Beth. They seem to be moving in their sickness at a slower pace. We also needed the antibiotics as well. Some sort of cough or bacteria was making its way through our basement. I don't know why it was. But all of us seem to be coughing just a little bit more.

We were ready to go. We had been preparing since the early hours of the morning. I told Kevin to stay in the cooler with my daughter and not let her leave his side. He agreed.

There wasn't a single one of us that got on that evacuation bus without a bag. We were able to pull from whatever we had with us and I just set a clothing. The basement of the restaurant became the improv of apocalypse ware. Tablecloths were cut for scarfs and facemasks. Freezer bags were placed over our shoes. Silicone cooking gloves on our hands three or four gloves thick. There were two coats in the freezer. The walk-in freezer. I took one and Joan got the other. I offered to share, and I guess the men were being chivalrous. Adina gave us instructions, very detailed instructions. I worried at first, I wouldn't remember until I saw Joan. While we couldn't use the phones to make calls or anything, she pulled out her voice memo and recorded everything that Adina said. They were a lot of items, and I worried about carrying them all. Then it hit me. The produce bin that we use for catering. It had a handle and wheels, it was a good size case. It would work and roll across the debris if needed. We could put the items in there and keep them relatively safe.

I was nervous about going top side, yet curious. We had no idea what was ahead of us. We hadn't seen any of the destruction. Only the aftereffects of what it did to people. I gave my daughter a hug and kiss goodbye, and along with the others I ventured up the steps.

I wanted it to be my job to pull the catering bin. Although I doubted, once we loaded it that I'd be the one pulling it on the way back to the basement. I knew it would be full and heavy as well, considering some of the items on the list that Adina gave us. Mark was confident he could find those items and knew what they were, that was, of course, if anything remained at the hospital.

We discussed what we would experience when we left the basement. Dark to light. The basement seemed less dark, and that told me my eyes were adjusting.

Mark had sunglasses in his pack and led the way up the stairs.

When he opened the door and tossed the bin through, he blurted out a soft, "fuck" I figured it was bright or smelled bad.

It was both.

It started before I even crossed the threshold of the basement door. I was last and I watched as Joan and Ted lifted their arms, moving blindly like prisoners released from solitaire.

"Look down," Mark instructed. "It will have less effect. Keep your eyes down."

Well I did that, and it didn't matter. It wasn't even that bright, but it was enough.

The contrast of stepping into day hit my eyes and they not only instantly watered, I went blind. It reminded me of when I got my pupils dilated at the eye doctors or coming out of a movie theater in the middle of the day, only worse.

There was no way I could move. I stumbled through the door, kept my head down and eyes closed.

The "Oh God" and groan of pain from Ted expressed what I felt.

Mark said something about carrying the bin out of the restaurant. I was fine with that.

We had to stay there in the kitchen though, not move until our eyes adjusted. It took a few moments, not long.

I almost wished I didn't have to see it.

If the kitchen was a small indication of the world outside the restaurant, I wasn't ready.

When I had left the restaurant, it was in it's usually prestige condition. The black and white checkered floor always spotless, were smeared with a gray substance. The pots and pans were everywhere, a piece of the ceiling lay sideways across the salad counter, and a huge section of the wall and the stove was black and charred

Bits of food were on the ground, open cans scattered about. But that wasn't where the smell came from.

I recalled that smell as the same one in the basement, it was now mixed with another and the moment I recognized it, I realized in horror what it had to be.

Death and decomposition had a rotten smell, indescribable, but the other odor that laced with it was sulfur.

As the last from the basement, I took the lead out of the kitchen.

Turning the corner from the kitchen into the main dining room confirmed my thoughts.

Ezzie hadn't made it far.

What looked like a puddle of slimy, blood laced vomit, was the beginning of a trail that not only led to an even bigger and bloodier puddle, but to Ezzie's body as well. She made it halfway across the dining room, dying on a pile of shattered glass from the windows and doors.

I turned my head slightly when Joan moaned out an, "oh my God"

I watched her whip the cloth from her face, back up and

vomit on the floor.

I thought it was the sight of Ezzie, but it wasn't.

I guess my focus was on the trail leading to Ezzie, and I didn't see until I watched to make sure Joan was okay.

The tiny baby.

He lay on the floor not far from the first puddle. The blanket has unraveled from him. He looked so tiny, helpless and sad.

I guessed in her desperation to flee the basement and die with her child, she didn't think about what the drain cleaner did to her. It left her not only horrendously sick, but unable to do the one thing she wanted to do, leave this world with the baby in her arms.

Her death was horrible.

It was evident by the mess on the floor and Ezzie's body.

I thought by drinking drain cleaner the poison of it simply would kill her. It was so much more.

I stared down to Ezzie, caught in some sort of bizarre mesmerizing moment. She didn't look real, she smelled it, but didn't look it.

Her lips and mouth were a greenish gray, the color covered her throat and her chest. Her clothing looked as if it had been burned off of her. There was a hole in her throat as well.

Mark must have noticed my engrossed stare.

"Drain cleaner has lye," Mark said. "It's caustic. It started eating away the moment she drank it. I'm surprised she made it this far. It destroyed her from the inside out."

"There were other ways to die." I said.

"This was the easiest I suppose," Mark said. "You alright?"

I repeated the word, "yeah" a few times as I nodded.

"Can we go?" Ted asked. "Please, can we go?"

A verbal answer didn't need to be given, after looking once more at Ezzie, I moved toward the broken front door.

At least a thousand times over the years, I walked from the restaurant.

I knew not to expect the same, but somehow I was still

shocked.

The street had been previously blocked off, it now had cars scattered about, tossed about from the force of the blast.

I was surprised the buildings were still standing.

Looking toward my right, toward where the blast would have come from, I could see more destruction, big piles of rubble. A dark gray, looming cloud hung over the destruction of the city.

I firmly believed the designs of some buildings saved them. Long structures with business store fronts were all connected. Every eight or so business began a new building, the first of the row took the brunt of the hit.

"Here," Mark handed me the handle to the rolling bin. "Or do you want me to pull it?"

"No, I'm good. Thanks." I took the handle, trying to figure out a path as we moved to the street.

The sidewalks were useless.

It was an obstacle course either way.

Furnitures, glass, chunks of concrete and bricks scattered about the road. That I expected, but not the vast amount of bodies. They lay not only on top of the mound of debris, but they seemed to be folded inside. Sometimes it was a whole body, but for the most part, arms and legs protruded, a face here and there.

Some were void of color, some covered in dry blood and some looked burnt.

"My God," Joan said. "Where did they all come from?"

"Yeah," Ted added. "There weren't this many people here when we ran from the bridge. They didn't all run after, did they? Why didn't they take cover?"

"They were probably on the bridge," Mark replied. "Or in their cars tossed from outside when the blast hit, some were carried a ways with the blast winds. Duncan and his dad were lucky that hadn't happened to them."

"We're they really lucky?" I asked. "Doesn't look like these people suffered."

"You don't always," Mark said. "We'll never know what they felt or knew, it's just sad."

We drew silent in our walk. Saving our breath, trying not to inhale too much of the air. The rattle of the empty bin hitting bumps was the only sound. I pulled it behind me, trying to clear a lane with my foot, scooting rocks and debris out of the way.

It wasn't long before we were to the street that was lined with busses waiting to take people out of the area.

Oddly enough the four of us who got on that bus together were now in a sense full circle.

The three block hike didn't seem quite impossible once the hospital came into view.

It was still standing, which was a good thing.

The windows of the north end of the building were completely busted and it appeared the top of the building suffered damage. We would know the shape the hospital was in once we got closer. I just knew that if we didn't have to, I didn't want to walk to Children's. Aside from being father way, it was so much larger.

Adina made it sound easy to find what we needed at West Penn. It was smaller, but it wouldn't matter if it was destroyed.

Every step I took, I kept looking for people. Signs of life or something.

There was none.

They had to be out there.

Maybe they were like us buried in a basement somewhere. Only they didn't have an Adina to help.

We weren't totally helpless. Admittedly, I knew some of the things that I had learned from the news and I was certain I wrote a lot in my notebook.

I just didn't need to retrieve it with Adina there. If I recalled, a lot of my notes dealt with long term survival.

Long term seemed ridiculous to think of, I was trying to just get through each day.

Maybe that was my problem. Like focusing on the hospital

in the distance and getting there, I needed to focus on the future of me and my daughter and achieving that.

Instead of baby steps to living, I had to take great strives so we could survive.

TWENTY-TWO – SAFETY

Mark had stopped twice as we neared the hospital, I questioned him neither time, but when he stopped again right before the entrance, I had to ask.

"What's going on?"

He peered over his shoulder at me, I was unable to read his expression because of the cloth covering his mouth. "Just … looks like footprints."

"Someone is here?" I asked.

"Was. I think. They look like they go both ways. In and out. Hard to say."

"I'm sure," Joan said. "Someone probably came for supplies like we are. Should we worry?"

"We should always worry," Mark replied. "Just be on your toes."

Ted stepped forward. "Unless they have a medical person, they aren't coming for what we are. I know I wouldn't."

"Me either," I said. "I'd come for other things. Actually, I would have hit Murphy's Pharmacy. It was still intact."

"Exactly." Ted nodded. "Probably didn't know where to begin here. We do."

According to Adina, she knew the hospital well and told us where to go when we entered.

The farther away from the windows we go, the darker it would be. Any emergency lighting would have long since passed its ninety minutes before they went out.

We were ready for that.

The lobby was dim, scattered debris and glass throughout.

There were two departments we needed to visit, and if time permitted, the Emergency Room. After listening to Adina's instructions once more on Joan's phone, we separated, putting a time frame on returning and meeting in the lobby.

Joan and Ted were headed toward a stairwell to make it to

the third floor. They were searching Oncology for a medication given to those being treated for Cancer and other items.

Mark and I had the first floor, radiology. The entire way there, Mark kept looking down, as if looking for more footprints.

It wasn't dark, the corridor was lined with broken windows and that gave us light.

In all my visions, not that I was psychic, but any time I thought of nuclear war, it looked nothing like the reality I currently faced.

The ceiling tiles had dropped, some lay on the floor, while wires dangled from the ceiling all down the hallway. That was a disaster event, not nuclear war.

It was hard to believe the bombs had dropped and Mark and I walked as an invisible killer seeped into our bodies with every tick of the clock.

It wasn't as bad as it could have been, maybe because we were some distance from ground zero.

"The hall will wind around, seems like forever but you'll get to radiology," Adina had said.

Sure enough we did.

I thought about how easy we found it and wondered about Joan and Ted. How were they faring? They had to go up two floors. We hadn't heard from them, so obviously they found a way up.

We entered the waiting room for radiology. A large spacious room with a huge window, which of course, like every other one was broken.

We found the corridor that led to the different imaging rooms, X ray and MRI.

As soon as we did, we pulled out our flashlights. It grew darker with each step we took.

"Find the diagnostics room," Adina said. *"It would be the room where they read the results. That's where the emergency exposure kit is and everything else you need."*

That wasn't hard to find, it was the only door that was

slightly open, and it was at the end of the hallway.

We tried to leave the door open to allow some light in. Propping it open with the catering bin.

The room wasn't very large and it had a pane of glass separating it from another room. That was the only glass I had seen so far that hadn't been broken. She had instructed us to find a metal cabinet that would be along the far wall.

"You'll see the exposure kit. It should be easy to spot. It will have all kinds of items in there. Check to make sure there is something called potassium iodide. It might be marked thyrosafe of KI. It won't help what me and Beth and Tim are going through, but it will help us not absorb any more."

Mark opened the cabinet, the doors of it were thicker and heavier than they looked. On the top shelf was a silver case marked CDC For Emergency Use Only. He unlatched the lid and looked inside.

I heard the rattle of the pills and he closed the lid.

"This is it," Mark said and handed me the case. "Put that in the bin,"

"Are you looking for the other thing?"

"Yeah."

I took the emergency kit over to the bin, as Mark shone his flashlight into the cabinet.

Adina had described what we needed as a long, black, narrow box. It would be heavy.

"I think this is it," Mark said, sliding a case from the cabinet.

"Just peek, don't look long," I told him. "Remember she said …"

"I know, I know, these are person meters, this box is shielding them from the radiation, and not to expose them. We need an accurate reading in the basement."

Mark set down his flashlight. "Come closer and shine your light in here so I don't have to leave it open long."

I inched forward aiming my flashlight.

He lifted the lid.

"Is that them?" I asked.

"Looks like it, yeah." He shut the lid. "Is that it?"

"No," I replied. "She wants us to grab a lead blanket to cover the items."

Mark nodded. "From one of the x-ray rooms."

"Maybe we can get a base reading there."

"Yeah." Mark lifted his light and shined it around. "I'm not seeing one in here."

Adina had asked us to get a base reading.

"Every room has one on the wall, she said, 'it measures radiation in case of accident. Get the reading. They are in MSV's. Or Millisieverts, don't be alarmed if the number is high. One roentgen is ten millisieverts"

We placed the case of personal meters in the bin and went into the next room on our way down the hall.

It was a basic x-ray machine and the door was extremely heavy. So much so, the bin would not hold it propped open.

"Jesus," I jumped when it slammed.

The flashlights barely illuminated the room.

"Search the walls," Mark said.

"I don't even know what it looks like."

"Maybe like a thermostat," Mark guessed. "Here's one of those blankets."

"Why are you not a cop anymore?" I asked, slowly moving my light left to right.

Mark chuckled. "That is really out of the blue. And strange because you don't make small talk."

"I was curious. You don't act like a cop."

"I'm not anymore."

"Did you hate it?"

"No, I loved it. I just couldn't do it anymore. My head wasn't in the game, so I moved to another level."

"I get that," I said. "What happened? Was it a divorce?"

"No, my um, my son died."

Hearing that caused a reaction in me and I dropped the

flashlight to the floor. "Oh my God, Mark, I am so sorry."

"It was five years ago. He was nineteen. Overdose. I was on duty when we got the call of a possible overdose and … it ended up being my kid."

My hands shook as I felt the floor for the light. "I'm sorry. I really am." I lifted the light and cringed. "I suck at small talk."

"How were you to know?"

"Maybe if I asked about your life. After all, we are all in this life changing event to…" I stopped speaking when I saw a square white unit in the back on the wall by the base of the machine. "I think I see it."

I walked over and looked. There was a radiation symbol and next to the digital displays were the letters MSV, "Yeah this is it," I said, looking at the reading. "And … its' broke."

"What do you mean it's broke?"

I tapped it. "It's broke. It says, point zero, zero, nine. Like nothing."

"Really?" Mark walked over to where I was. "I see that." Like me he tapped it. "Maybe we should try another … oh."

"Oh?"

"Yeah, oh. It makes sense. It's not broke. This room is built to spec. Meaning it has to have lead in the walls and doors to prevent radiation from seeping out in case of emergency. Makes sense it would stop it from seeping in."

"That can't be right."

Mark shrugged. "That's the only explanation. I mean, the door was closed, there are no windows, it's center of a brick building. The digital display is still on, so the unit works."

"That's amazing." I said in awe. "Every room should have a similar reading."

"The ones that are sealed with machinery, I guess."

I nodded. "We should go." I reached for the lead blanket in Mark's hand., I wasn't ready for the weight of it and I nearly dropped it. "Heavy."

"Uh, yeah, it's lead."

Hearing that made me pause and I swung my light around.

"What are you doing?" he asked.

"Looking." I moved about the room following the beam from my flashlight. "Let me get this straight. We're staying in a basement that smells foul, is dirty, a death cave, full of germs all because being there, underground, is safer when it comes to radiation."

"Yes. And what are you looking ..."

"Found one." I lifted another lead blanket and took it to the bin.

"Henny, we only need one."

"No, I need two."

"For what?" he asked.

"For my daughter. To cover her. Protect her. Once we get the stuff back there, I'm packing up supplies. According to that meter, we are in no more danger here, in this room from radiation than we are in that basement. And it doesn't smell. People aren't dying all around us."

"I get that. But what about the others?"

"It sounds cold, but I don't care what the others do. My first priority is to my daughter, to keep her safe and alive. This room, this place right here, can do that. And when we get back," I said. "I getting my daughter out of there."

TWENTY-THREE – LESS ONE

The definition of insanity is doing the same thing over and over and expecting different results. Or so I had been told. By that definition, Mark was insane.

He told me at least four times what I planned to do was wrong. That being in the basement was more than likely safer and I'd see once we got there and pulled the personal dosimeters from the lead case. His words were not going to make me change my mind, nor was him telling me I wasn't thinking it through.

So, I settled for passive nodding.

"Okay, Okay, I'll see what the gadgets say."

He kept saying the monitor in the back room could have been wrong.

I doubted that.

Even though I went into three different imaging rooms, read the meter on the wall and all of them were only a few tenths of a points difference, he still insisted.

We made our way back down to the meeting place in what I thought was impressive time. We were only gone fifteen minutes at most, but Joan and Ted had not returned.

I tried not to worry, considering they had to go to the third floor, and finding the medication wasn't as cut and dry as it was for the things we were to get on our search.

We waited a few more minutes then sought out the emergency room. Halfway there, Joan and Ted emerged from the stairwell. It sounded so loud when they burst through, I worried something was wrong.

Mark and I stopped and spun around.

"Where are you going?" Joan asked, her arms were full.

"We were headed to the ER," I replied.

"No need. We got everything upstairs," she said. "Saline bags and everything."

"Bandages, too," Ted added.

I walked closer to them. Ted looked pale, he was breathing heavily. "Are you alright?'

"Yes, just a little out of breath."

"From coming down the stairs?" I asked.

He shook his head and coughed. "No, we went up."

Mark stepped forward. "Up where? Higher than the third floor."

Joan nodded. "As high as we could go."

"Why?" Mark asked.

"We needed to see or try," Joan answered. "You know, see the city."

"And did you?" I asked.

Joan drew in a slow breath. "Yeah. It was very shrouded by a cloud, but the outline was there. What was left of it."

"It looked more like a shadow," Ted said.

I closed my eyes for a moment.

"See," Joan said. "I took a picture."

My eyes popped open. She took a picture? Did she seriously say she took a picture?

"You took a picture?" Mark asked, shocked.

Joan held her phone, her fingers maneuvered on the screen as Mark leaned in. "You have to zoom, but if you look close you can see."

"Oh, wow. Holy shit."

"Heartbreaking." Joan showed me the phone. "Henny, do you want to see?"

"Maybe later. Right now, we should get back," I said, tugging the bin, I moved forward by the others.

"By the way," Mark said. "Henny wants to leave."

"We know," Ted replied. "We're following her."

"No," Mark repeated. "She wants to leave the basement."

I stopped and turned around, facing Mark. "Why do you sound so much like a tattletale right now? I have no plans on keeping it a secret."

"I'm not tattling. Whether you believe it or not," Mark said.

"We're in this together. All of us. We got off that bus together."

I kept walking, stepping out of the hospital.

"I'm a little lost," Ted commented. "She wants to leave the basement. Where's the issue? We all have to leave the basement and the area. We can't stay. I was actually thinking a little further out we may be able to find a car or something. Head north. Maybe Lower Burrell, they took in evacuees."

"I'm not talking about her leaving the basement in a week or so," Mark said. "She wants to leave the basement ... today."

"And go where?" Joan asked.

I didn't say anything I kept walking.

"Here," Mark said. "The hospital."

"I'm confused," Joan said. "Henny, you're level headed. You obviously have a good reason. Can I ask what it is?"

"Yes. But not now." I said. "We shouldn't be talking at all out here. The more we talk the more we breathe in."

"Can we talk about it later?" Joan questioned. "When we get back and get settled?"

"Yes. And I have a good reason."

"Make it quick," Mark said. "She doesn't sound like she'll be down there that long."

I stopped walking. "Why are you making this so personal?" I turned around. I just wanted him to stop the conversation. At least right then. I just wanted to get back to my daughter. Ready to blast him again, I paused when I looked beyond him. Trailing behind was Ted.

Ted was coughing and while his coughing had become common place over the last day, this was different. He stopped moving, his back bounced heavily in the coughing fit and he whipped the cloth from his face.

"Ted? You okay?" I stepped his way, looking at Joan and Mark. "Something's wrong with Ted."

After letting go of the bin, I hurried my way to him, but before any of us could react or reach Ted, he dropped to his knees, then like a tree, fell forward, face first to the ground.

◇◇◇◇◇

"I'm not getting a pulse," Joan said.

"I found one," Mark replied.

"You sure?"

"Positive."

There wasn't time to do CPR or administer any care. We were still two blocks from the basement and the only medical person around.

Had it not seemed so serious, I would have opted to take him back to the hospital.

Ted was out of it. His eyes were open, yet slightly rolled back. His face had taken on a greenish gray appearance. His lips and fingers were blue.

He wasn't a big man, so we sat him on the bin back against the handle and hoped for the best as we all worked together and moved the bin.

We moved it as fast as we could.

Once we got to the restaurant, barely through the open doorway, Mark grabbed hold of Ted and placed him on the floor.

"What are you doing?" I asked.

Mark leaned over Ted. "He's not breathing."

"Oh my God," Joan gasped.

Immediately, Mark started administering breaths.

"Mark, stop," I said.

"Do you need my help?" Joan asked.

Mark shook his head.

"Mark, he's dead," I told him.

"He's not dead," Mark said in between breaths. "Why can't I get …" he spoke frustrated. "Air into his airways."

'Are they blocked?" Joan asked.

Mark kept trying.

"Are you even doing it right?" I asked. "I mean, you're not doing the chest things."

"Compressions," Joan corrected. "And he has a pulse, he's just not breathing."

I watched how diligently Mark tried to revive Ted. It was a mission to him, one he didn't want to fail. One, I felt was impossible.

I stepped closer. "Mark, listen to me. Let him go. He's already gone and …"

It was the oddest thing, like a snapping sound. I watched Ted's chest rise as it filled with air. A second later, Ted wheezed loudly and burst into a coughing fit.

I stood there shocked.

"What were you saying?" Mark looked at me and helped Ted to his feet. "Come on, buddy, let's get you inside." He slung Ted's arm over his shoulder, then braced Ted under his arms. As he led him toward the kitchen, Mark turned his head and glared at me. I would have sworn he added, 'fuck you', but he didn't, he only glared.

Watching him drag a semi-conscious Ted toward the kitchen I wanted to yell at him that the poor guy was barely alive again, and to give him a chance, but Mark looked as if he had no patience for me.

Joan and I lugged the bin down the stairs, it was heavy, and we were pummeled with that smell the second we were mid way down the stairs.

We set it down, Mark helped Ted into the cooler.

"What's going on?" Adina asked. "What happened to Ted?"

"He died," I said.

"He what?" Adina asked in shock.

Joan explained. "He went down, Mark had to do breaths on him."

Adina brushed by us and went to the cooler.

I decided to follow to see if Ted was alright.

Seated outside the door was Van.

"Why are you out here?" I asked.

Van exhaled heavily. "Sick. Guess I didn't dodge the bullet after all. Not as bad as …" he pointed to Tim. Feeling a little puckish."

"I'm sorry," I said. "Hey, we got that medicine though. Let me check on Ted and I'll be back."

When I walked into the cooler, they had about four lanterns lit, and Adina was standing over Ted. He sat on a crate propped against the wall.

"I just … I just couldn't breathe," Ted said,

"Dude." Kevin blurted out. "I told you not to go out there, didn't I?" He shook his head and walked over to a book bag, he unzipped it. "Just as I thought, you didn't even take it." He held an inhaler and gave it to Ted.

"You have asthma?" Adina asked Ted.

Ted nodded and took two puffs of his inhaler. "Been pretty bad the last day, But … I'm almost out of this and I am conserving. This was more than my asthma though. I felt like I coughed and whatever I coughed up was stuck in my airway, I feel better now. A little weak."

"You need oxygen," Adina told him. "And another inhaler."

Ted looked up at Mark. "Thank you for saving me."

"I wasn't giving up on you," Mark replied then stared at me, which in turn made everyone look at me.

"Okay, okay," I held up my hands. "I wrote you off. I admit it. That was my bad."

While they gathered around Ted, I checked on my daughter, then left the cooler for the bin full of stuff.

Beth was coughing nearly as much as Ted had been. Tim thrashed a bit.

Jeff the window guy kept calling out, "Who's there? Who is it?"

I wondered if it was the sickness or the basement that was giving them a level of delusion.

Trying not to respond to them, I opened the bin.

I knew exactly what I needed to get out of there.

I opened up the lead case and pulled out one of the small boxes inside. The box was marked personal dosimeter, I pulled it up from the box and removed the warning label that said once the seal was broken it was not to be reused.

I pulled the seal tab on the back and even though the words were tiny and unreadable, I could make out the picture instructions and held down the little green button.

After a few seconds it beeped, the digital display flashed twice then went solid on a zero, decimal point, zero.

It worked, I hoped.

I took it with me to the back of the basement near the Pittsburgh Toilet so I could change into my uncontaminated clothes that I had waiting there.

Joan was already one step ahead, changing hers.

It felt like a high school gym class for me, changing clothes quietly.

"Here," Joan taped me on the shoulder.

I looked over.

"Before you dress." She handed me a pack of baby wipes. "I found these in a drawer at the hospital. Can't be any more exposed than what we're using down here."

"Thank you." I took one and the first thing I did was wash my face and neck. It felt so good and cool. I swear it blocked out any smells for a second. "This is wonderful."

"I thought so, too."

"Ted has asthma, you know," I said as I washed.

"I didn't know."

"Only Kevin did."

"I know a lot about people down here, I'm surprised I didn't know that."

"Do you know about me?" I asked.

"Your daughter talks a lot." Joan smiled.

"I know very little."

"Habits are hard to break," she said. "You're a guarded

person. I get that. That's fine. That's who you are."

"I never was one for a group mentality."

"I figured as much," Joan said. "So, do you want to tell me why you want to go back to the hospital?"

"I want to protect my daughter. I need to keep her as healthy as possible."

"Fair enough."

"I want to pack a bin with some supplies, enough for however long we have to keep hiding out."

"And some," Joan said.

"And some. Maybe once I am there, I can actually start thinking about what will be next. Like Ted said, maybe I'll head to Lower Burrell."

"You still didn't tell me why you want to go back to the hospital. We have Adina here, how is taking Macy away from a nurse keeping her healthy?"

"Radiation," I replied.

"It's everywhere."

"Not there."

"You're mistaken," Joan said.

"I could be. I could be wrong. But they had meters on each wall of the radiology department. Each room. Like a mini thermostat. They measure radiation in case it escapes."

"Okay." Joan nodded.

"Each of them was the same. Each of them read within a tenth of a point or hundredth of a point of each other. And it was low, it was like incredibly, almost nil low."

"How is that possible?"

"You know how they give you a lead blanket when they take an X-ray?"

Joan nodded.

"There's lead in the walls. There's lead in the walls to protect radiation from seeping out in case of an accident. It works both ways."

"Oh my God," Joan said with a little shock. "And you want

to go into one of those rooms."

"With my daughter, yes. It can't be too much longer until it drops to the level Adina said."

"She said a safe number is two roto something an hour."

"Which we don't know when that will be until we do the math."

"Nine more days," Joan said. "I did the math already. I'd give it a full two weeks."

"Then that's how long we'll wait it out there."

"Won't it be safe here?" Joan asked. "I am not discouraging you. But I would think being underground It'd be safer here."

"I did tell Mark, that I would see how much radiation we're getting down here."

"So, you found those meters?" Joan asked.

"We did."

"You know they only measure what you're absorbing not what's in the air. The number will never decrease."

"Yep. I know." I nodded and lifted the dosimeter. "That's why I …" I paused when I saw the display.

"What? What is it?"

"How many of those radiation things can we absorb until we start to get sick?"

"Adina said a hundred or a thousand of the other measurements." She pointed to the dosimeter. "What's it say?"

"We've been back here what? Five minutes? It's almost one now." I showed her. "We can absorb a thousand of these? How long until we get there."

It was a rhetorical question, I wasn't expecting her to answer. But Joan was the math person and after a beat she spewed out. "That's twelve an hour, nearly three hundred a day."

"Assuming that it didn't drop from yesterday, which we know it did, I'd say we already hit that number. It's only a matter of time before we're …"

Tim groaned loudly in the distance.

"Hopefully never that bad," I finished. "I don't want to

chance it."

All I wanted to do was get dressed, get my supplies and get my daughter out.

The numbers said it all.

TWENTY-FOUR – VENTURE

There was no more debate in my mind what I was going to do. I grabbed another catering bin, one that hadn't been outside, and started filling it.

Water, food, tablecloths, some lanterns. In fact, I knew it was going to be heavy so I took the bin upstairs carrying items up the steps to fill it.

My initial plan was to put Macy in one of the bins and cover her with a lead blanket. That way she would be as protected as I could get her.

I realized it wasn't going to work. We needed supplies and I was only one person.

We needed food and water, which would be what I had to carry in the bin.

It was only a couple blocks.

I was a woman on a mission, carefully calculating what I would take. I didn't have a plan beyond that stay at the hospital, I'd work on it.

Ted sat in the cooler, a tablecloth around his shoulders covering him. He looked somewhat better. Adina was giving him a lot of attention.

"Do you realize what you're doing?" Mark asked.

"I do," I replied. "I showed you the dosimeter. Another day down here, I won't be able to stop my daughter from getting ill. Why are you taking this so personally?"

"Because you put me in a hell of a predicament."

"What do you mean?" I asked.

"I came into this basement with you. I got on that bus … with you. Whether you like it or not, we are a team and you're leaving. Yet, I feel responsible for the people down here."

"I can't help you with that."

"You brought them here. You argued for them," he said.

"I did what I could. Now I have to worry about my

daughter."

"What about your safety? I'm not talking radiation. I'm talking people," Mark said. "There is safety in numbers. You go alone and you are taking a risk."

"She's not alone." Kevin stood up. "I'll go with her. I owe her my life. If she hadn't let me out of that police car, I'd be dead. Can I go with you?" he asked.

"Yes, absolutely," I replied. "Anyone can go with us."

"So, we're just going to abandon these people," Mark said.

"I'm not abandoning anyone, I'm worrying about my daughter and getting her to a safer spot," I argued. "All these people can come. I don't care."

"They can't," Adina said. "Three are too ill. However, Ted needs things we can only get at the hospital."

"What if we get the things?" Kevin asked. "And I bring them back."

"Oh, I'm fine," Ted refuted.

"No, you aren't," Adina said. "Your fingertips tell me you need to be on oxygen. You need another inhaler. Because of your asthma your immune system is compromised."

"If it's compromised," I said. "Wouldn't he be more susceptible to radiation?"

Adina nodded.

"So why doesn't he come to the hospital with us," I suggested. "You tell us what we need to do for him, and we will."

"How are you going to get him there?" Mark asked. "You saw how much trouble we had with him on the bin."

"I'll walk," Ted said.

I looked at him. "You're not walking. What about … what about a dolly? Strap him to a dolly." I spun to Kevin. "Do you think you can push him the three blocks?"

"Sure."

"No!" Ted snapped. "He'll drop me."

"Dude, I won't drop you," Kevin assured him.

"What do you think?" I asked Adina.

"I think those who are healthy enough to go, should go," she answered. "Get to a safer, cleaner environment. I'll give you all the instructions you need. When we are well enough, we'll join you."

I looked at Adina, it was clear she was ill. Sores had formed around her mouth, and her skin look spotted.

I knew those of us who sought refuge in that cooler and weren't exposed when levels were high, looked healthy. It needed to stay that way.

It was settled for the others.

Joan decided to stay back and help Adina. I understood why because Adina wasn't well enough herself to handle how bad it was going to get.

There was a short debate between her and Mark on which one of them would stay back. For our safety, Joan suggested he come with us.

Kevin said he could keep us safe. I found it kind of insulting that they thought I was incapable of protecting my daughter and myself.

It came down to Mark compromising and saying he would go to the hospital but would check on those in the basement.

Since there were more of us going, that meant more supplies, and admittedly, having Mark help with that was a blessing.

It would require a couple of trips, which he would do, while I got things situated there.

The first of which would be to help us get our stuff there, then return to the basement with a wheelchair for Ted, because he just couldn't see us rolling him across the debris in a dolly.

It was time to leave.

We began to pack what we needed and had decided to take.

The place that was our original sanctuary was fast becoming our death trap, and it was definitely time to go.

TWENTY-FIVE – SAFER HAVEN

Macy's face said it all. Her expression encompassed what we all were feeling, it summed it up perfectly. When she emerged into the world above from the basement, when her eyes had adjusted and she could finally see, her little eyes widened and then glossed over as her brow furrowed and her lips pouted in a fight not to frown.

It was Kevin's first emergence as well.

His youth was never so evident as it was when he saw the destruction.

I wonder if we held the same look when we saw what happened to our city. Staring at the desolation that represented what we felt.

Mark was ahead of us, trying to get to the hospital first to get a wheelchair and return for Ted. He moved faster than Macy could move with the lead blanket. I wanted to put her in one of the bins, but we had too many supplies to bring.

I held her hand as I tugged one of the bins. Kevin beside us and Joan behind us. She decided to help us carry things before she returned to the basement.

"I'm sorry, sweetie, for what you're seeing." I told her. "If you want to close your eyes you can. Just hold tight to my hand."

"No," she replied, shaking her head. "It's okay. It's not that bad," her voice trailed off. "It's not that bad." She looked left to right then back up to me. "It could be worse, Mommy."

For a split second, I couldn't imagine how it could be worse. Then I saw the bodies again on the ground, mixed in with the debris.

That could have been us.

When we finally arrived at the hospital, Mark was making his way out with a wheelchair. Not that he was impatient, he just wanted to get back and get Ted.

"Can you see if you can find oxygen?" he asked me. "I'm sure somewhere there's a cylinder."

"I'll look," I replied and nodded.

He said he'd be back shortly, and I expected that to be true.

I figured I would get Macy in one of the imaging rooms, put our supplies in the diagnostic room.

Before we went into the dark rooms, I looked at my dosimeter. It read one hundred and one. I had absorbed in that short span, ten percent of the 'sick' number, and that was only since having the meter. I didn't want to think about how much radiation I had taken in before it.

I placed Macy in the one room, checked the reading on the wall unit, it hadn't moved or changed since I had left.

After putting a personal dosimeter on Macy's shirt, I set her up with a couple little lanterns and went to help Joan with supplies before searching out the oxygen.

"You know I heard on the news," Joan said. "While they were giving instructions, that if you didn't have a basement to find a windowless area, or center of the house. Like a hall. I guess harder for the radiation to reach you. Makes sense in here." She looked around. "No windows, these rooms are interior rooms, for lack of a better word."

Kevin's voice entered the room. "That makes sense. You know in the 1950s all schools had to be designed with a windowless core. A center that was stable. For tornados and bombs."

"How did you know that?" I asked.

"I wanted to be an architect," he replied.

"You were in college?" I asked.

Kevin nodded. "Does that surprise you? I told you that when we first met."

"I'm sorry that time was foggy. I didn't remember. You don't seem like the college type. More musician or artist." I said.

"Architecture is art. Not to say I got very far. I was only first year. And ... if you guys are okay, there's something I need to check." He pointed back.

I barely got an 'okay' out and he was gone. I wondered what he had to do. Maybe he was taking it upon himself to look for oxygen. I didn't know exactly what he was up to, but a few minutes later, Kevin shined.

Literally.

It was only about four inches by four, but the little LED light was the brightest we had seen in a dark room since the bombs fell. The yellow tint of the flashlight and lanterns was replaced by an almost clinical looking light.

"I found three. I already gave one to Macy," Kevin said. "You should have seen the smile on her face."

"Kevin, where did you find them?" I asked.

"I know for a fact the code says the emergency lights have to be operational for ninety minutes, well, it's a hospital. They have a backup plan to a backup," Kevin said. "I got these from the receptionist in the lobby and one from the check-in here in radiology. There are more. Probably two or three at each nurses' station, not to mention the OR."

"That's really good thinking," I told him.

"Something I remember my mom talking about, plus, I need one to search for her locker."

"Is this where she worked?" Joan asked.

Kevin nodded. "Yeah."

I stepped to him. "I know you want to find that locker. Can you wait another day or two? Just give the radiation a chance to drop. Adina said it effects the young easier than those older."

"I get that," he replied. "I do. But I can help here. I know where they keep things. Like the oxygen we need for Ted, and the inhalers. If I promise to hurry, can you let me do this? I need to do this. I have been in that basement doing nothing. I just want to contribute."

Joan asked. "Will you be fast?"

"Very," Kevin answered.

"Then Henny and I will sort through what we brought. You

go." Joan grabbed his hand. "Go find your mother's locker and oxygen, then get right back."

"Thank you." Kevin backed up.

"And ..." Joan stopped him. "If you find any more of those LED's ..."

"I'll grab them, I promise." Kevin hurriedly turn and raced through the door.

I looked at Joan. "I was going to guilt him into not going."

"I know you were, but our mental state is as important as our physical one. He needs to find something of his mother's."

I suppose she was right. Kevin just seemed so young to me, and I worried about him. I checked on Macy once more, she seemed fine and content, then I returned to the diagnostic room with Joan and we sorted and separated the supplies we had brought, waiting on not only Kevin's return, but Mark and Ted as well.

◇◇◇◇

Kevin had returned with the oxygen and inhalers, long before Mark and Ted arrived. I found a blanket in the closet and made Ted a bed on the MRI table while Mark walked Joan back to the basement.

The tubing for the oxygen was sealed in a bag, and the inhaler was in a box. Ted was so grateful for that inhaler, and the oxygen seemed to be doing him some good. Adina had instructed to feed him a slow flow of oxygen until his fingertips no longer looked blue.

By the time we had things settled it was evening. And I appreciated those LED lights.

I made Macy a plate of peanut butter on crackers and sat with her cuddled in the corner of Image Room three until she started to doze off.

I switched from the harsh LED lighting to the softer table

lanterns and only used the flashlight when I checked Macy's dosimeter.

"You know," Mark said. "Watching that dosimeter is like watching a pot of water. It's not gonna change if you keep looking at it."

"Good," I told him. "I don't want it to change. Mine has changed enough."

"She'll be fine."

Finally, I looked up at him. He had a backpack on his shoulder and he stood nearer the door. "Why do you look like you're going somewhere?" I asked.

"I am,"

"Back to the basement?"

"No. I ... I had a thought. You know, this was a big evacuation point. People came here and waited for a ride. They had to have had a shelter plan."

"What do you mean?" I asked.

"I mean, they had days warning on the bombs, right? They had to think, what if they didn't move all the people out, what if people were left behind?"

"Do you think they set up a shelter?"

"That's my train of thought. I think I'm going to take a look. If they made one, it's somewhere here."

"Center of the building."

"Or lowest point," Mark said.

Carefully, I moved Macy from my lap and stood.

"What are you doing?" Mark asked.

"I'm coming with you. At the very least, we can salvage things."

Mark didn't argue or tell me to stay back, he handed me a flashlight and said, "Let's go."

It was after we left the radiology department that I realized how dark it was. There was no longer any daylight, no matter how gloomy, coming through the busted windows. I used the wall as a guide, trailing my fingers against the surface.

Mark walked ahead of me.

At first, we walked in some sort of awkward silence. One I had to break.

"Hey," I called to him. "I'm sorry."

Mark stopped and turned around. "What for?"

"Me and you, we really got off on the wrong foot."

"Well, considering our first encounter you ran into me, fell and blamed me, then the second time you slammed the door in my face."

"Yeah." I cringed. "I'm sorry."

"It's okay."

"No, really, it isn't. That's not who I am."

"It isn't?" Mark asked.

"Excuse me."

"Not a dig, honestly, I'm not tossing a dig, but you are pretty closed off. You don't really warm up to people."

"I've warmed up to everyone through this."

Mark just stared.

"Alright, not you. Let's ... let's start over." I extended my hand. "Henny. Nice to meet you."

"Mark." He shook my hand. "I think we met. Not sure. A little over a week ago. But you were kind of busy, so was I. In any event, nice to meet you, too." He paused. "Feel better? Less guilty?"

"Not really."

Mark chuckled.

"You seem like you know where you want to check," I said.

"I do." He lifted the flashlight to a sign that read, 'parking garage'.

"You think that's where they are?"

He nodded. "It has three sublevels. Yeah, I do."

"What about the basement?"

"If they brought supplies in, they'd have to bring them where it is easiest to unload. The basement isn't. If they brought in supplies." He aimed the sign. "The parking garage is it."

TWENTY-SIX – CREASE OF LIGHT

"Bingo," Mark said.

It was like a black hole, something out of a horror flick. I never knew anywhere could be so dark. We were swimming in a void, guided only by the flashlights. I had nothing to hold on to, no wall. It was weird how vulnerable I felt.

I kept commenting that I felt like I was in some sort of horror film, more so, zombie movie, where something was going to come out of the darkness and get us.

I stayed close to Mark, hating how scared I was.

Then the beam of his flashlight caught it. It reflected off the plastic wrapping. Another twenty feet we would have hit a wall … of supplies.

The plastic wrap covered the pallets of water, four of them from what I could count. There were other pallets as well, it would take getting close to read what they were. But the clear water bottles absorbed our lights.

I smiled. "I can't believe this. How did you know?"

"Just from being a cop," he replied. "I did emergency response and was on duty for a lot of hurricanes. Give me tomorrow, I may get the generators up and running."

"That would be great."

"Now … let's see what we all have." Mark started examining. "Looks like four pallets of water. There's seventeen hundred bottles per pallet."

"We need math whiz Joan."

"Yeah, we do." He moved down the line. "Meals Ready to eat. Oh, yeah, blue mats."

"Excuse me?"

He showed me. Through the plastic it was hard to see exactly what it was. All I saw was a spot of blue.

He explained they were emergency foam mattresses covered in a blue vinyl material. An easier replacement for the cot system.

They were stacked on a pallet as well.

"Henny, there's enough here that we can sort through this over the next couple days, figure out what we need. We can't stay in this area."

"I know."

"I think what Ted said. Head toward Burrell, or north. Farther away from the city."

"Won't everyone that survived be doing that?" I asked.

"Leaving the area? I don't know. People are creatures of habit. Look at Hiroshima. They all stayed in the city."

"Because they didn't know better."

"True." Mark let out a breath. "Okay, so ... what do we need?"

"Nothing right now. Wait until light. Even though it won't get any better down here with daylight. We can at least bring the rolling bins."

"What about we take some of these blue mattresses? It'd be nice to sleep on something."

"That's a good idea."

"Here, hold this." Mark handed me his light and crouched down. "Just aim it down here for me. I don't want to remove the entire ..."

He stopped talking.

"What is it?"

"There's a light."

"What? Where?"

"Coming from the ramp that goes below. I didn't see it until I got down here. It's not real bright."

I crouched down as well and peeked. It was faint and across the garage, a slight glow emanated from the level below. I stood. "Do you think there are people?"

"Has to be. Come on. Stay close."

Was there really any other choice? The line of pallets had blocked us from seeing that light, but once we made it around, it was hard to miss, and it was a guide for us to follow.

Halfway across the garage, there were empty pallets and plastic wrap. But there were no sounds. Surely if there were people, we'd hear something.

Maybe it was just one person or two.

We made it across the garage and as soon as we turned the bend to the ramp, it was brighter. The flashlights weren't even needed.

Quietly and slowly, we started our descent, but we only needed to make it midway. Once at that point we learned it wasn't just one or two people, it was an entire group.

Rather it looked more like a survivor camp.

Those blue mattresses were placed neatly on the floor with emergency lights set up sporadically.

The cots were filled, people lay on them. Some were sitting. There wasn't that sound of groaning and moaning of people suffering.

And there wasn't any smell.

From what I could see the level was clean and neat. Someone had organized the survivors.

Mark looked at me. "Let's go down there."

I nodded and took a step.

"Stop," the firm male voice said. It came from behind us. "Don't move."

I slowly looked over my shoulder to see a man holding a rifle on us.

"Don't take another step. Do it and I promise you," he said. "I will shoot."

TWENTY-SEVEN – ROLE REVERSAL

It was a different type of fear, staring at the military looking rifle. Although I didn't know much about weapons, it certainly looked like one someone from the military would carry. But the man holding it didn't look military at all. He wasn't in any uniform nor looked to be in very good shape, and he looked to be about fifty.

Despite the fact that we were in the midst of post nuclear annihilation and it was dark, he looked impeccably clean.

Even though he looked like a somewhat good guy, I was still scared. There I was, surviving a blast only to die after being shot.

"We aren't here for trouble," Mark said.

"Set down your flashlights slowly," the man instructed. "Then raise your hands."

I did as instructed, keeping my eyes on him. "We aren't armed," I said.

"Yes, you are," Rifle man replied.

"No, we're not," I insisted.

"Yeah," Mark said, "Yeah, we are."

"We are?"

"I am," Mark said, "I have my pistol,"

"Why would you bring a gun to look for supplies?"

"I don't know, Henny, maybe in case there is trouble."

"Oh, now there's trouble because it looks like I lied to the …"

"Hey," Rifle man snapped. "Enough. I know you aren't here for trouble, I heard your conversation." He lowered his weapon, then shouldered it.

"How much trouble can there be?" I asked. "I mean, really, down here."

"You'd be surprised what people can do when they're

desperate. How long do you think it'll be before looters come out?"

"After three days?" I asked in disbelief.

"After three hours," he said.

"People panicked and were desperate before," Mark said. "You remember the last few minutes, right?"

I nodded then looked to Rifle Man. "If you know we aren't here for trouble why are you threatening to shoot us?" I asked.

"Because I can't have you go down there," he replied. "None of those people have been topside since the bombs. None of them have seen more than an inkling of radiation. Look at you." He shined his light on us. "Both of you are covered with dirt and I gather ash. At least you have your shoes covered. And your hand." He moved the light to my left hand. "You better decontaminate now or you're gonna be one sore puppy in a few hours."

I glanced down to my hand, my fingers were covered with some gray substance. I rolled my fingers together feeling the course ash. I couldn't figure out how it got there, and then I remembered, the wall. I held on to it, feeling it as we walked in the dark.

"Jesus, Henny," Mark lifted my hand.

"I didn't think." I shook my head.

"You obviously have a place where you're hunkering," Rifle Man said. "You said you don't really need supplies."

"Not now," Mark said. "Maybe for when we leave."

"Do you know where you're going?" he asked.

Mark shook his head.

"Do you have a radio?" he questioned.

"No," Mark answered.

"So, you have no idea where to go, no radio to find a place, nor do you even know how you're getting there?"

"That …" Mark lifted his finger. "I have given thought to. What about you?"

"We have a plan," Rifle man answered. "I'm taking it

there's a lot more of us than you. How many in your group?"

"Upstairs right now," Mark replied. "Five. But there's nine of us altogether. The other four are at our previous basement shelter."

Rifle man nodded.

At first, I couldn't figure out where he was getting nine from. Adina, Van and Joan only made eight. Then I remembered Beth wasn't as exposed. Even though Duncan's father and window man were close to passing, she wasn't.

I asked, "How did you manage to be down here?"

"Well, supplies were dropped off just in case this had to be an emergency shelter. When we realized the buses weren't coming, or even if they did, we'd not get out with the traffic, we started setting it up."

"Upstairs no one is sick," I said. "In fact, I have my daughter up there. She's nine. The only exposure she had was when we came here and I covered her with a lead blanket. We won't bother you, if you can just let us have some of those blue mattresses, I'd be grateful, we've been sleeping on the hard floor."

"You have a kid up there?"

"Yes, yes, we do, and like I said, no one is sick."

"The sick thing is not true," Mark corrected. "Ted and his asthma."

My eyes widened. "I'm not lying to you on purpose, sir."

"Sir." He scoffed a laugh and shook his head. "Call me Devon. And ... I can't make any promises, let me go talk to my people down there. See if we can make room for you. Especially with a kid. Maybe if we get you decontaminated. We have a good clean set up."

"We'd appreciate it," Mark said.

He gave a nod, turned and went down the ramp.

After a pause, I looked at Mark. "Do we need to go down there?"

Mark shrugged. "Can't hurt. We've been in so much filth

and stench, that might not be a bad idea to go somewhere healthy for the remainder of our wait. Or your wait. I promised to go check on Adina and the others."

"I know you did." I let out a heavy breath.

"Kinda ironic, don't you think?"

"What is?" I asked,

"A few days ago, we were safe below deciding the fate of those above us. Now we're the ones whose fate is being decided."

"Is our fate really being decided?"

"Every better place is a better chance for survival."

That made some sense to me. I thought I had found a safe place for Macy. Maybe below where there they were set up like a camp, would be even better for her.

I vowed to protect and keep her safe.

We waited for what seemed like an hour, but it wasn't. It couldn't have been.

I imagined them weighing the decision. Suddenly, we were the ones that were radiated, we were the ones that would bring filth, sickness and smells into their tidy area.

Devon returned, and I knew by the look on his face what the answer would be.

"They would rather you not," Devon told us. "They just don't want to take any chances."

"Understandable," Mark replied.

"I argued that we could use the help with keeping watch. It's not all that bad though. Here's what we came up with. These supplies are public. They don't just belong to us and there are plenty of supplies. Our suggestion is; leave your contaminated stuff up wherever you have it and move your group to this level. It's still safe, we'll get you some decontamination stuff, a radio, too. We'll help as long as you help us in keeping a watch on this place. You can make a nice area on this level."

"Thank you," I said.

"And … another thing. They'll allow the little girl down

below. Her and you," He looked at me. "That's it."

"Well," Mark said. "There you go, Henny. You want to keep your daughter safe. Here's your chance. We'll get Macy and bring her down."

Something inside of me sparked an immediate response of, 'no', I gave a polite smile to Devon. Not that I didn't want to keep my daughter safe and protect her, but at what cost? Leaving those who stood by us since the beginning.

"No, but thank you," I told Devon. "We'll stay on this level. That is generous of you. I want to stay with Mark and the others. We'll do what we can to help you out as well."

"I get it. I do," Devon said. "I'll get started on getting you those supplies. We're a radio call away. And I'm sure one of us will help if you need it."

He glanced at my hand, and I caught the worry and concern he projected. I got a feeling of dread, like he expected it to get bad, immediately that made me worry, though I said nothing, I just rolled my hand into a fist.

"And the offer stays open for your daughter," he said. "A lot of us were hospital workers that never made it on a transport. We have family …"

Suddenly his voice faded in my head.

My mind started spinning, a million thoughts pummeled me. I saw his lips move, but hadn't a clue what he was saying.

For some reason, my body moved passed Devon, and I rushed to the ramp.

"Hey!" Devon yelled.

"Don't shoot me, I'm not getting near," I replied as I hit the ramp. "I just need to get close enough to yell."

I made it a little further than halfway down the ramp when the camp came into my view. It truly was set up neatly. Long tables sectioned off different areas. There had to be at least fifty people.

I felt my arm grabbed, then heard Mark's voice. "What are you doing?" he asked.

I jolted my arm away and hollered out. My insides shook, it was crazy, but I had to try. "Is there a woman here who has a son named Kevin?" I paused. "Or do you know a woman who has a son named Kevin? She would be a nurse. He's young. First year college. He's a great kid. He is looking for his mom. She worked here. Anyone? Is there a woman here who has a son named Kevin?"

There was ruffling of people moving around, staring at me. No one said anything.

"It's okay," Mark laid his hand on my back. "You tried."

I nodded sadly and prepared to tell Devon I was sorry. In defeat, I peeped out one more, 'Anyone' before starting to turn and that was when I saw her.

A woman stood up.

"I do," she said. "Please tell me this isn't a trick."

I slowly shook my head, conveying that it wasn't.

TWENTY-EIGHT – NOT INFALLIBLE

It didn't matter to her that she risked contamination after being sheltered and safe.

She was a mother who desperately wanted her child.

I felt it, I saw it and I totally understood.

I prayed we hadn't misled her.

"Where is he? Where's my son?" She grabbed ahold of my arms. "Please tell me where he is. Is he alright? Is he hurt? Sick?"

I wanted to give her all those answers, but I shut down, fear took over that it might be nothing but a coincidence.

Despite the fact that she wanted to come with us back up to the hospital, Devon convinced Denise, or Nisie as he called her, to just hold tight.

Stay put, help pull supplies and wait.

They gave us two lights to make our journey much easier through the dark halls.

On the way back to the radiology department, Mark and I discussed going and getting Joan and the others in the morning. Bring them back, give them a chance with a safe shelter, one that was clean with other medical professionals to help guide us in their care.

That would be when daylight arrived.

Until then, we had to get Macy, Ted and Kevin.

I wanted to blast to Kevin that we found his mother, but I refrained, simply scared that if I was wrong, I would be breaking two hearts.

Kevin was the biggest whiner of them all when we told them what we wanted to do.

"What's the difference? Down there below or up here surrounded with lead," Kevin said. "And we just got Ted to stop coughing. If we move him, he'll start coughing again. And Macy is sound asleep."

Mark winced a little listening to Kevin's excuses, then he explained. "From what we saw it was supposed to be a shelter camp. There are supplies there. Clean supplies and a way for us to get the radiation particles off us."

"A lot of good that would do," Kevin said. "We would have to put the same clothes back on."

"I think they have suits," Mark said. "You'll be able to get out of those blood stained and sour smelling clothes."

"I smell sour?" Kevin asked.

"Yeah, you do. It's worth the walk down there. Trust me. We will be much better off physically waiting it out down there," Mark told him.

I kept quiet. Scared to death I'd slip and say something about Nisie.

I just hurried them along. We left everything but the dosimeters behind. I was just glad we had all covered our shoes with the sani-booties. We needed our shoes.

With just the dosimeters on our persons, sani booties on our feet, we made our way there.

We didn't tell them others were down there, nor did we tell them they didn't want us with them on the lower level.

In a sense, I was relieved.

I remembered how I felt about Adina and the group when they joined us. Suddenly we were the cause for the smells, sickness and noise.

Even if it were no fault of our own.

Now here we were exposed, and even though we took those pills that block radiation absorption, we stood a chance of getting sick, while they on the third level were the healthy ones, looking at us the way I looked at Boris.

"Is it going to be better, Mommy?" Macy asked me as we walked.

"I think so, it'll be brighter and cleaner. And since we have to stay below for at least another week and a half, it's the best place to be," I replied.

"Like we said," Mark added. "Plenty of good stuff, too."

"I'll tell you," Ted coughed after he spoke. "Getting those two lights, knowing about new clothes and decontamination, you guys must have really found a treasure." He paused for a coughing fit. "You weren't gone that long."

"See," Kevin said. "One minute in this dust, away from the oxygen, he's dying all over again."

"Oh my God." I looked at Kevin. "He's not dying."

"I could be," Ted said.

"You're not dying," I told him.

"Mommy, is Ted gonna die?"

"No." I widened my eyes to Kevin. "See. Stop."

"I can see," Kevin said. "Thanks to those lights. But they aren't oxygen."

"There's oxygen there. I'm sure of it," Mark told him. "Lots of other things, too. Including a radio so we can call out."

"Call who?" Macy asked.

"Anyone," Mark replied.

"What for?"

"To see what's out there. Eventually find a better place, one we can stay at," Mark said.

"Is there one?" Macy asked.

Her simple question brought silence, even to Kevin. And it stayed that way, until we crossed from the hospital wing into the garage pay lobby, then finally the staircase.

"We're walking down to two," Mark instructed, leading the way down the very dim stairwell.

"Why not three?" Kevin asked, "There are three sub floors. Why stop at two?"

"We have the supplies on two."

"Why can't we bring them to three?"

"No, why so wound up, were you eating sugar?"

That comment made me smile. Kevin did seem hyper. Maybe subconsciously he knew things could turn good for him.

Like a kid at Christmas, he continued to ramble fast. "I

would think the farther we go down the better." Kevin paused. "Wow, that coughing sounds even worse in the stairwell, Ted. It's loud."

"Everything's loud," Mark replied. "Walking ... talking."

"Are you saying I'm loud?" Kevin asked. "It's just the echo in here and ... do you hear that?"

Mark had nearly reached the second level. "I can't hear anything with your mouth working."

"Sounds like someone is running. You don't think they're running to attack us, do you? Like in Mad Max. Footsteps against the ..."

The second sub-level door to the stair well swung open with a bang, causing not only Kevin to scream but Macy and myself as well.

Lit by Mark's LED light, Nisie stood there in the doorway breathing heavily, she heaved out an emotional and relief filled, "Kevin!"

"Mom?" My guess was because he was behind me, he didn't see her at first, only heard her, but it was enough to send him barreling through the darkness. Clumsily making his way by me and Macy, and after nearly tripping when he reached the second level landing, he grabbed hold of his mother, almost knocking her over as well.

With all the bad that had happened, the depressing thoughts, the darkness, finally, I witnessed something good. Something uplifting, and for the first time I felt a little hope for what was ahead.

◇◇◇◇

Devon had to be frustrated, but he hid it well, only grunting and getting a little snippy once and a while.

I suppose Nisie broke the stay safe rules.

But, hey, it was her son.

She was overwhelmed to see and hold him, rightfully so. I could only imagine the fear as a parent she must have felt and the relief to find out he was alright.

"What happened to your face?" she asked.

Hearing her ask that, I forgot how bruised he was, and that his head was sutured by Adina.

"It's fine, Mom, I was stuck in a police car," he told her. "I was trying to find you, they forgot about me. These people ... her." He pointed to me. "Henny, especially, she saved me. She helped me. If it wasn't for her, I'd be dead."

Nisie briefly stopped holding her son to walk over and hug me.

"Oh, goddamn it," Devin said. "Quit touching the contaminated people, please."

She chuckled, then spoke softly near my ear. "I will never forget this. Ever."

"It was all of us," I said. "We're a group."

Lips tightly closed, she produced a partial smile and stepped back. "You gave me my son. I'll always be grateful."

Maybe her premature gratefulness was the reason they just didn't give us a space, they gave us much more than we expected.

By the time we had returned, they had set up a small perimeter of lights, encircling what would be our little camp placed in the far corner opposite the ramp going down.

Little blue mattresses were neatly stacked waiting for us to determine how we'd set them up, blankets were in sealed plastic bags, and a square white table was there as well.

Before we entered the area, we had to decontaminate.

It was for our own good.

We did so on the other side of the room, taking water from this huge container, rinsing, then washing with this special soap, and rinsing again.

We wore these outfits that reminded me of light colored

hospital scrubs. Ted said they were more like prison wear. But they felt fresh and comfortable, for the first time in days I think I relaxed.

I set up Macy next to me and she was the first one examined and given a clean bill of health. Nisie for some reason felt it necessary to bandage my hand and fingers. It didn't make sense to me, they didn't hurt and were only a little red from irritation.

To top it off, she put both me and Mark on an Intravenous drip.

"No arguments," she said. "Devon said to do so. You're dehydrated and the medication will help your body process any radiation you absorbed."

"Devon?" I asked with surprise. "He said to do this?"

"Yeah, he knows best."

"Really?"

"Devon was the chief of staff at the hospital. When he was practicing, he was one of the best oncologists in the business."

"Wow. I would never have known. I thought Devon was the maintenance man."

"No," she shook her head. "He was the big wig. Like the captain, he stayed with his ship. So, he says IV, you get an IV." She placed the final strip of tape over the shunt. "Kevin said you already took potassium iodide tablets?"

"Yes," I replied. "The thyro something or other. We took them right after we got back from the hospital and again before we left to come here."

"Good. Good."

"Why aren't Kevin, Ted and my daughter getting an IV?" I asked.

"They may," Nisie replied. "Right now, by my assessment, the doctor wants you and Mark on the drip. Humor us."

She made me relax on the mattress next to my daughter. I just didn't get it. I felt fine. I liked her, she was a warm woman, young, too. She promised to stay on our level with us. Others below offered as well. Kevin speculated that they were so healthy down below that all the health professionals were bored.

The world didn't seem so bad in that garage. Not near as bad as it seemed in the basement. It smelled better, we smelled better. We ate a warm meal and drank juice.

The next day, or when we got the medical go ahead, we would get Joan and the others.

I dozed off for a little bit, it was the first quiet night since the bombs dropped. I hadn't a clue how long I was sleeping when I woke up. My IV bag was still half full, my mouth was dry and I downed some water.

My hand started to itch pretty badly, I attributed it to the bandages. Grabbing my small flashlight, I rolled over to check my daughter. She was curled on her side, the blanket over her shoulders as her head rested on the paper pillow. I inched over to her as much as I could and reached for her dosimeter. Using the flashlight, I checked the readout.

"The boiling water thing," Mark whispered.

"Yeah, it's not boiling. That's a good thing." I released the dosimeter, kissed Macy then sat up carefully on my own mattress. Mark was seated on his right across from us.

"How are you feeling?" he asked.

"Good. Tired. My hand is itchy. Guess it's the bandages."

"Hopefully it won't get that bad, right? I mean we both have these IVs," His eyes shifted downward to the tubing. "It's supposed to help get the radiation out of us. Devon said we shouldn't get as bad as Duncan and his dad, or even Boris. He has meds in case we need it to feel better. That's a good thing."

"Yeah, that's a good thing." Admittedly, it was an automatic response. What he said hadn't sunk in, when it did, I hurriedly looked at him. "Wait. What? Why would we get bad? Why would you say that?"

Mark lifted his dosimeter.

When he did, I grabbed ahold of mine. I had forgotten about it. I honestly didn't give my dosimeter a second thought. I illuminated my meter and read the digits, taking in a sharp breath.

"This can't be right," I said.

"It is."

Neurotically and constantly I had checked Macy's. Maybe subconsciously, somehow, I thought looking at hers constituted looking at my own. That her numbers would be the same as mine. But they weren't. She had been protected. I wasn't. I was out more, I had touched the radioactive dust on the walls. It never dawned on me how much I was exposed. Had I just looked at mine every time I checked hers, I wouldn't have been so ill prepared when I discovered how high my absorption numbers actually were.

TWENTY-NINE – BIDING TIME

When I woke up the next morning, my hand had swollen to the point I couldn't move my fingers, and even if I could, I didn't want to. The burning sensation was so severe, it felt as if it reached my bones.

I focused on that pain, it kept me from dwelling on the headache, nausea and stomach cramps.

My absorption of radiation came mainly from the dust I had touched.

Mark's was more from exposure, and he fought showing how ill he felt as much as I did.

While we wanted to leave and check on Joan and the others and give them a radio, we couldn't. We couldn't risk taking in anymore radiation.

So, the following day, an older male nurse, named Walter, from the third sub-level volunteered to go. He brought them stronger medication and a radio.

I felt useless again.

Funny thing about radiation, it doesn't work the way one would think it would work. I always believed once you get poisoned with it you immediately get sick, and you either get better or die. Not that I ever thought much about it before my crash course of survival by watching the news or listening to Adina.

That only happened in acute lethal doses of over ten gray or 100 roentgens. We believe that was what Boris, Jeff, Duncan and Tim all had.

Less lethal doses of four to six gray worked differently. Sickness within days, sometimes hours, and then the person feels better … for about a week or so, then more severe symptoms would kick in. They either get better after several weeks or they die.

That is the dosage Devon believed Van, Adina and Beth

received, since, even though they were sheltered, they were above ground for the first four hours. The heaviest time for radiation.

Radiation lesson two point five came after Walter radioed to say Van was doing better.

I was relieved to hear that.

"General rule of thumb," Devon said, "With the exception of those who receive a fatal dose, the faster you get better, the higher the dose you received. With lower levels your body tries to process it, get rid of it and fight it. With higher doses it processes and fights what it can and stores the rest, that is the reason for the second round of symptoms."

So, there was a chance Van could still get sick again.

Devon felt the need to explain it to me again, using the term 'my friends', trying to give me comfort and some sort of reality when Walter stated Beth wasn't doing all that well.

Truth was, they weren't my friends.

Most of those nine people who joined us were just names.

Names that meant nothing to me. Like secondary characters in a book that pass by in a scene, or red shirts in a television series brought on to just to be killed.

Like the reader or viewer, I felt nothing for them, I wasn't invested in them enough to care and that was just sad.

They were faces that came into our shelter and added a burden.

Just like I was to the people on level three.

A nameless, face that was sick and needed help.

The world had fallen apart. Millions, if not billions, had died, and I couldn't take the time to know the few that lived around me?

No wonder karma was delivering a radiated blow to me.

The memories of people, who they were and what they did, was all we had left.

Millions of deaths would be in vain if no one was to remember a name, a face or a story.

I had survived.

There had to be a purpose for it other than just to protect my daughter.

If there wasn't a reason, I'd make one.

It wasn't too late.

I didn't want to be a nameless, faceless person. I didn't want my daughter to remember the bombs and how her mother didn't care about anyone or anything but her. From that moment on, I vowed to change. No one else would be nameless or faceless to me. I would do what I could to remember a name, a face and the story of every person I met.

The buildings were gone, life as we knew it ... gone.

The memories of those who lived in this world and their contributions didn't have to go, too.

We all had to make a difference, and I would do what little part I could.

For my daughter's sake, I needed to make sure she knew civilization may had died, but humanity hadn't.

THIRTY – LOOSE ENDS

In a way it was a good thing that boredom set in. The hours that slowly slipped by, the confusion on whether it was day or night.

They all kind of just lumped together.

I tried to keep as much structure as I could for Macy, sleeping at night, staying awake during the day. Trying to get her to do some sort of activity, whether it was reading, writing or drawing.

It was difficult because I ended up going down for the count. Not due to the radiation sickness, I was handling that, my hand, however, was a different story.

The burning turned to blisters, which then transformed into sores, which eventually ended up as ulcers.

There were times I just wanted someone to cut it off. When I felt like screaming and crying, I refrained simply by thinking of those in the basement and how they had cried out.

Mark had more dignity with his illness than I did. He kept going, helping when he could, moving items, counting, and dropping with his stock, 'My bad'.

I knew when he was feeling really bad because he would disappear for a spell. I always believed it was to throw up or nap in a corner without looking weak.

I wished I was like that. Sadly, I depended on my daughter.

She brought me water and cool clothes, wiped my head and cuddled when I felt horrible.

I was supposed to be protecting and taking care of my daughter, but she ended up being my own private nurse. She was so strong, I envied her.

There were two other children there, I wished she would try and make friends with them, but she stayed by my side.

Like mother, like daughter, I guess. But I stayed true to my word. I was able to finagle a logbook from Devon and I took notes on the people I met. No interviews, just interesting facts. Did they have family, were they searching for someone, worried about someone?

Who knew, maybe in the future we'd run into them.

I took notes.

I started with Beth.

When Van, Adina and Joan arrived four days after we settled into the garage, Beth wasn't with them. She had passed away.

I asked what they knew about her, I honestly wanted to know, wanted to care about something in regards to her. Unfortunately, she was the wrong person to start with.

In Adina's words, "She really had no redeeming qualities."

She wouldn't go into details.

I just made a note that she died, and no one liked her much. I guess my logbook needed negative as well as positive. After all, good and bad is what made us human.

And there was bad out there, fortunately, we hadn't encountered it yet.

Joan told about seeing groups of people salvaging from stores, she refrained from using the term looting. She, Adina and Van waited outside before heading into the garage because they didn't want to be seen.

Eventually the city and urban areas like Bloomfield wouldn't be safe at all.

We would have to leave.

To go where, we didn't know, or even how we would leave.

Other than Ted talking about growing plants and food, nothing about the future was discussed. The radios were useless outside of our garage. Even the bigger radio failed to reach anyone.

Our plan was to head out after nine days, but we stayed below. On day sixteen, on the day I started feeling like myself again, we discussed the next step.

I think the big reason it wasn't talked about was the problem of moving sixty-three people.

Not only moving them, but where to go.

"Some of these people have family," Devon said. "They want to search them out. Others, well, this is it."

"Where do we move the others?" I asked. "We can't stay down here."

"We are our own community," Mark replied. "There are enough people down here to start our own camp."

"Find an area," Ted added. "Start building from there. Plus, really, think about this. The government had warning. There's a plan. They're out there somewhere, they'll emerge again."

"Do we want to wait for them?" Mark asked. "Sit down here and wait for looters to find us?"

"Like I said before," Ted stated. "Start with the evacuation centers. That would be the first arm of the government. Head there"

Sarcastically, I asked. "Just load everyone up and move on out or create some sort of post apocalypse pilgrimage?"

"That won't work," Devon said. "Loading us all up will. But realistically we need a destination."

"We need a scouting group," Mark said. 'Transportation though, is gonna be an issue. We can't walk, even with low radiation that's dangerous."

"The theory is," Devon said. "Anything running when the bombs went off won't run again due to the EMP. Cars not running when the bombs fell may. I have my car on the level above. The scouting party can take that."

"And the others?" Mark asked. "A bus won't be easy to find."

Interjecting in the conversation was Kevin. He had been listening and stepped forward., "Liberty Bruce Motors."

We all looked at him.

"Liberty Bruce," he repeated. "A buy here, pay here place five blocks away. I bet it's still standing. Small white building, the cars are all in the lot, the keys to the cars are in a cabinet behind the one desk. That's how I got the car to get my mom."

"So, you did steal it?" Mark asked. "Like the cops said. You told us it was a friend's car."

"I did. I didn't want you to think you helped a thief. I'm not. In a way he was a friend, I was trying to get a car there before the bombs."

Mark grumbled. "Okay, so we can ... steal ..." he looked at Kevin. "Some cars for the group once we know where we will all go. The scouting party takes Devon's car, if it runs. The radios may not reach any camps, but they should work between us. We send out a group to find a destination. Radio back when we do."

"We?" I asked. "You're volunteering?"

"I am," Mark replied. "These people helped us. It's the least I can do. I'll head out first and keep them posted along the way. Let them know what's out there."

"Count me in," Ted said. "I'm ready to see what's out there."

"Me, as well," Joan added.

I didn't say it at the moment, but in my mind, I knew Macy and I would go along, too. I would be raising my hand and saying, "Us, too."

The garage offered a level of safety, but for how long. I knew it was risky taking my daughter, but unlike the scouting mission to the hospital, I couldn't leave her behind.

Not this time.

Whoever went out with the first group to leave the garage wasn't coming back, they were finding a place, whether they were waiting for the others or not.

Mark, Ted, Joan, Kevin and I were all strangers the day the bombs fell, but we had turned into more than that.

Three of them were leaving, I had no choice but for me and Macy to go along with them.

We started this journey together.

We would continue the journey together. I didn't want it any other way.

And it was time to leave the safety of the shelter and finally face what was left of the world.

THIRTY-ONE – EMERGE

Taking Devon's expensive SUV was great in theory, but that went only as far as the ramp to the street level. I was glad common sense kicked in with us before we loaded up only to be stuck.

The amount of debris, thrown cars and bodies, along with broken glass made it impossible to even try.

We ended up using Kevin's Liberty Bruce Motors idea and siphoning gas from Devon's vehicle.

Mark went out with Walter the nurse to find a car and get it as close as they could.

Walter was a good guy. He was one of the survivors that had family out there, just outside of Cleveland, he said. He was a traveling nurse.

They made several trips to get the car and load it.

In the government supplies there were handheld radiation readers, or Geiger counters as Devon called them.

The levels had dropped to seven point eight millisieverts per hour or less than one rad.

Safe enough to move about outside for a limited time.

They found an older and unattractive station wagon. Though not the best thing on the eyes, it ran.

Kevin made a comment that he only saw older cars in every apocalypse movie.

Thinking about it, he was right. I always assumed it was a budget issue with the studio.

While they made the trips to the geek wagon, me, Macy and Joan moved up to the first level ramp with our supplies. It allowed for our eyes to start to adjust to the brighter surroundings. It also allowed me to see how truly pale we all were. I hadn't looked at my own reflection in a long time, nor did I want to. I knew how I felt, I was only now starting to get stronger. If Joan and my daughter, who were healthy as horses, were pale, I probably looked like death.

I know Mark did.

It would change once we emerged into some semblance of ultraviolet light.

We tested the radio several times with Mark, it worked well, and we held high hopes it would keep us in contact with Level Three, the radio code name Mark gave them.

Ours was the Road Warriors or RW, the giving of nicknames made no sense, we hadn't heard anyone on the radio other than ourselves.

For three days we soaked our old clothes to disinfect them and get them clean. It felt strange putting jeans on again after essentially wearing pajamas for weeks.

The clothing, radio tests … the car… it was time to move out.

Twenty days after the bombs were dropped. Time enough to heal, feel better and mentally prepare.

There was no definitive plan, our only plan was to get on the first available roadway out. We had an idea of where to go, we were focusing on the evacuation centers. That was it.

We would radio along the way, like live stream broadcasting.

Van was on his feet and stayed behind with Adina who had ended up knowing a few people on Level Three.

Kevin decided to stay back with his mother. That wasn't a surprise, I would have been surprised if he didn't.

I felt this strange unexpected sadness when I said goodbye to him. Not a feeling of foreboding, just sadness that I was leaving him.

I guess despite what I believed, I cared a lot more than I thought I did.

I embraced him whole heartedly. He thanked me again for that first day. My mind flashed back to him in the back seat of that police car, his face bloodied and eyes so lost.

We all said our goodbyes, but kept them short, in my mind

and heart we would see everyone again.

"Remember," Devon told as we prepared to leave. "Don't be deceived. Try to avoid being out for long periods of time, check your dosimeters often. Especially after you get farther out. You aren't leaving the radiation, you're chasing it."

Chasing the radiation.

It made sense after thinking about it. The radiation moved with the jet streams and wind.

As Devon described, like spreading peanut butter, if you start out with a glob, the glob gets smaller as you move the knife, but there is still a glob.

We were headed into the glob. Or at least running behind it.

Emerging back onto the street wasn't as much of a shell shock as it was the first time, at least visually with the damage and destruction. But we emerged into a totally different beast of a world then we did days after the bombs.

A much colder and grayer world. The dust from destruction had seemed to permanently cloud the sky. It was July, and the weather felt like fall. There was no wind, no sound, it even felt silent.

I looked for people, the looters that Joan had told me about, I saw no one.

If they were out there for days, more than likely, they were sick somewhere now or worse, dead.

Even with the tacky station wagon loaded, we still carried supplies.

Macy held my hand, looking around, studying her surroundings. She wasn't buried beneath a lead blanket that served as blinders for everything around her.

I could feel her little fingers tensing around mine every time we passed something horrifying, and we did often.

As we walked down the street closer to where Mark had placed the car, I saw evidence that people tried to survive. Somehow believing that if they stayed just inside the store fronts they would be safe.

Their lifeless bodies huddled around each other were like a tragic window display.

There were more than I thought.

If they just would have gone into the building or below.

Ignorance makes for a hard call, especially when dealing with something like nuclear war.

None of us ever believed it would happen, we never bothered learning.

Why would we?

But it had happened.

Those who died in front of the broken windows believed they were impervious to danger as long as they were sheltered.

Just like I thought I could run my hand down the wall without repercussions.

I wasn't just touching dust, I was touching death.

They weren't breathing air, they were breathing poison.

An invisible poison that cut right through them.

I was so grateful when we finally arrived at the car.

We loaded the rest of our things in the back of the wagon and got inside.

Mark would drive first, he and Joan sat up front. Ted, Macy and myself in the back.

"Ready?" Mark asked, his voice sounded shaky, he was as nervous as the rest of us.

No one replied, there was no need. It didn't matter if we were ready or not, we were in the wagon and perched to go.

Mark started the car.

THIRTY-TWO – MOVE AHEAD

The sound of a baby crying in the distance filled the air, it wasn't a newborn, they had a distinctive cry. This was a young child unable to verbalize what was wrong, what hurt or if they were hungry.

I heard that cry for the longest time. Listening from the car trying to pinpoint where it came from. Did we pass the baby, or were we approaching it? Maybe the world was so quiet the sound of the cry just cut through.

I prayed that there was an adult with him, that someone was trying to tend to the baby's needs. Common sense told me that after three weeks, somebody had to be taking care of the baby.

Were they still there?

We moved at a slow pace going northeast. The houses and building were farther apart, the road less covered with debris.

As we moved to the end of the neighborhood, the crying stopped.

The dead silence returned.

"Someone is holding him,' Ted said softly. "Someone has the baby."

When he said that my heart broke thinking about all the children out there who lived through the bombs, the ones that didn't know not to go outside.

The ones that were alone crying in sickness and pain.

It made me hold my daughter a little tighter.

We checked in often on the radio, probably more so to make sure we still were in range and we still had communication with the others.

I just wanted us to move, to be able to drive faster without the painstaking slow pace that seemed like we were on some tour of Hollywood homes. With the tour guide announcing every sight.

"*And over there you see McDonald's, the staple of America*

fast food. It's gone now. If you look to your right, where the family of three is sleeping, that used to be Mosely's car shop. Good old Mosely was on an evacuation bus, right smack on Bigalow Boulevard when the bombs fell."

The good thing about moving farther from Bloomfield was people. We did see more people.

They camped out in small parks, on the sidewalks. I stared at them and they stared back as we drove past.

None of them looked any better than us, they were pale, sores on their faces. Some had lost hair, some were burned. They huddled around garbage cans of fire trying to stay warm.

What were any of us thinking? The amount of energy I expended trying to learn and get out of the city could have been spent finding a spot far enough away and below, waiting it out.

Did I actually think the traffic would miraculously move and I'd be free from the bombs?

I should have known better, we all should have known better.

Finally, we made it from the side, finagling our way to Butler street and to the 62nd Street bridge. I honestly didn't think we'd make it over. I feared, like the Bloomfield Bridge, it too would be packed with traffic.

Apparently, that evacuation route was clear.

It was frustrating to me, all that time sitting on the bridge simply because I needed to get to the campsite south of the city, when my main concern should have been just getting out.

The open roadway had only a few abandoned cars with doors open. I suspect the drivers took off running when their car stopped.

The trees that lined the road, the overgrowth of foliage was all dead. Winter dead.

I didn't see another car, and I looked behind us.

"Stop," I said to Mark.

"Why?"

"I … I have to see."

His eyes met mine in the rearview mirror and he slowed down, then stopped.

"Where you going, Mommy?" Macy asked.

"I need to see, Baby."

"See what?"

"The city."

I knew the stretch of roadway well, I knew it was the bend that when coming from the north the city came into view.

We all stepped out of the car.

There was a world of difference from seeing the picture on Joan's phone.

It was real.

Though far in the distance, the top of the skyline was different. The triangular skyscraper had been reduced to two beams, I'm sure there was more remaining, but from my vantage point it didn't look like it. Jagged edges and shadows made up the rest.

"It will never be the same, Mommy," Macy said, grabbing my hand.

"No, baby, nothing will ever be the same."

I felt sadness and overwhelming anger. It wasn't an act of war, two countries taking it too far. It was one entity deciding the fate of humanity.

Taking a bright future away from my child and replacing it with darkness and danger. This wasn't the world she was supposed to inherit.

I hated that I had faced it.

Those who did it thought they won.

Maybe they did.

In my mind and heart, we as a people had to do everything we could to steal that victory from them.

It didn't start with government or military, it started with people.

They destroyed our buildings, but they didn't destroy us.

Not yet.

THIRTY-THREE – WHAT WE DO

The signs started to appear just after the Freeport exit on Route 28. We talked about going through Freeport, but with the evacuation center only a few more miles away, we opted to aim for it. It had to be big, it was set up in the state's largest mall.

First came the signs, then came the survivors.

We started seeing them on the road walking in that direction. So many of them calling out to us, asking us to stop.

For what?

Where would we put them?

It wasn't like a massive exodus of people, more of a steady trickling that led all the way to the roundabout road that encircled Pittsburgh Mills Mall.

When we first arrived, we saw nothing that looked like an evacuation center, no indication that people were even there. Then as we drove around toward the other side, we saw a bus, a couple of military trucks. Finally, when we passed the sporting goods store we saw tents, rows and rows of them.

But we didn't see that many people.

"I'm thinking we don't drive right up," Mark suggested. "Let's park back here with the other vehicles and walk to see what's going on."

It was a good idea, and we parked by the bus, almost hiding the station wagon.

"Level Three," Joan called on the radio. "You there? Can you hear us?"

A second later, Devon came on. "We read you."

"We made it up twenty-eight," Joan said. "Evacuation center is at the Mills Mall. Looks operational, although not seeing many people here. Saw a lot, I'm assuming, trying to make it here."

"People are emerging now around us," Devon replied. "Probably seeking help. Let me know what you find out."

No sooner had we all stepped out than we were approached by a soldier.

"Can I help you? Entrance to the camp is that way." He pointed.

"Thank you," Mark said. "As you can see, we drove. We didn't know where to park. Thought it was better here. Is there someone in charge?"

The solider looked at Mark curiously. "Did you need something? There are different people trying to keep it together for different things, there are different aspects of this place. Some of you look like you might be sick."

Mark shook his head. 'Actually, on the mend."

"That's good. What did you need?" he asked again.

His question made me pause. What were we doing there? Really, what did we need?

I simply blurted out. "We just have questions. That's all. We don't really need anything."

"I don't know how many answers anyone has, but I'll show you who you may talk to."

He took us to a man that I expected to be frazzled, no real reason to think that, I just imagined with the camp being so big everyone would be beside themselves.

He wasn't. He was actually pleasant and composed. He was in a tent alone, it looked like an office, and he was separating items out of MRE's when the soldier brought us to him.

He introduced himself as Edward then said, "Glad to meet you folks. Give me a second, I'll get your information." He walked across the tent. "I'm making boxes. I heard there are a lot of people on the highway." Edward grabbed a clipboard. "Okay," he said, exhaled and sat down. "If you don't mind being together, and you're just passing through, I can give you a tent that's already stocked. Then again …" he reached out and cupped his hand on Macy's chin. "This little one looks pretty healthy, good job. I would choose the north entrance, that's our family area. Keep her indoors. Find a store, a set up, we'll do what we can."

I looked at Mark, he looked at me. We all kind of looked at each other.

"Okay," Edward said. "What am I missing? You're here for refuge, right?"

I shook my head. "More so information."

"Oh." He cocked back. "Okay. What can I help you with?"

We hadn't planned for an interview. "You're still here after three weeks," I said. "How many people are here?"

"I lost count. Close to a thousand now," he said. "When the evacuation happened, we had triple that amount. Right after the bombs a lot of people left. Maybe to look for family, to see if their homes were still there. A week later, a lot of people returned. Sick. Now that seems to be the majority of what we get. Those sick with radiation and injuries."

"So, you're helping the sick?" Joan asked.

Edward sarcastically laughed. "If that's what you want to call it." He pointed to the main entrance behind him. "Right through there is where the sick are. Unfortunately, we don't have enough hands to help everyone. We do what we can. They keep coming, but we really aren't equipped to help. We aren't a medical set up."

Mark asked. "Have you heard anything about the government? Are they still operational? Are things getting back on their feet?"

He shook his head. "I haven't heard anything. That's not to say something isn't in the works. Just we haven't heard anything. It's only been three weeks. If you folks don't need space, why are you here?"

It was a strange question we weren't expecting to be asked. I know I didn't have an answer. None of us did. We set out to find a place where we could all go. None of us really thought of what that entailed.

We radioed back to Level Three, then opted to stop, see

what the camp was about, maybe come up with the next course of action.

The evacuation camp was still running, others would be, too.

We decided to stay in the family section, even if it was only for the night.

There was a play area for children, and the kids there ran around playing and laughing. A new normalcy I suppose. The parents set up homes in the stores. We set down our belongings in a former phone store.

Joan and Ted offered to stay with Macy as she joined the other children, and I sought out Mark.

He didn't come with us to find a place.

I'm glad that I did look for him.

I got to see first hand what the mall had been transformed into.

In the family wing, or the north section of the mall, stores had turned into mini homes. Some people looked as if they took the three weeks to set up a permanent place, using furniture from stores or curtains. There weren't as many people as I expected or hoped.

Like Edward said, the majority were sick, and he wasn't exaggerating, in fact he downplayed it.

It was heartbreaking.

Ted had told me Mark was with the truck. I walked through the mall to get to that exit.

The closer I got to the center, I started seeing people in the corridors, laying there, sitting there. It was like a stream that led to a river and the river to an ocean. That ocean was the center of the mall.

The food court and event area were filled with people. Tables moved aside to make room for the makeshift beds on the floor.

There were a lot of those blue mattresses, but more so people slept on the floor. They lined the halls. Sick and coughing, the smell was there as well.

Sounds in tenfold that were reminiscent of the basement. Only there were more crying children. The most gut wrenching victims of the entire event.

When I was younger, I had watched a documentary on Hiroshima. One of the pictures that had stuck in my mind was one of a large building filled with victims of the bombs.

The mall reminded me of that.

I didn't see a single health care worker. One or two people walking around, maybe checking on the ill. No one really attending to anyone. Nobody administering care. No IVs, no medication, just suffering.

It was far too much.

My mind started spinning and I started thinking.

This was our world now.

Dying. Like the people in the mall.

They had a big beautiful safe structure, but they didn't stand a chance.

Kevin stood a chance because we helped him out of that squad car. Adina, Van and the others, they stood a chance because we brought them to the basement. I stood a chance because Devon and the others helped me.

The sick, mall people ... didn't stand a chance. No one was there that could help.

Stepping outside was a welcome relief.

Mark was organizing things in the back of the station wagon when I found him.

"Hey," I said on my approach.

"Hey." He shut the hatch. "Come to get some fresh radiated air."

"Something like that." I Inched closer. "So, is there a reason you aren't inside?"

"Yeah, I um, just don't feel comfortable leaving our only means of transportation out here and vulnerable. Too many people."

"Most of them are coming here because they are sick and have nowhere else to go."

"I still don't trust it."

"What are we doing?" I asked.

"What do you mean?"

"What are we doing? We packed up, we left to do what?"

"Is that sarcastic?"

"No, I'm serious. I just don't know what it is exactly we're doing?"

He leaned against the back of the wagon. "My understanding is that we were leaving to find a place to go. But I'll tell you Henny, this mall isn't it. Right now, everything seems fine, because everyone is still shell shocked. They're rising from the ashes, sick and worn down. But in a few weeks' time, it won't be that way. There is very little organization, people are left pretty much to run in packs."

My ridiculing laugh interrupted. "Packs, like animals?"

"Yes, like animals. No authority in there. It's like a prison without guards. It will erupt."

"Wow." I blinked a few times.

"Look, okay that's harsh and I don't blame Edward or any of the other four people that are working here. What can they do? Maybe if they had help, things would be different. They aren't. They don't have the hands."

"What if they did?"

Mark looked down at me curiously. "Are you suggesting we stay?"

"Not entirely," I said. "I'm suggesting we make a difference."

"What the hell does that mean?"

Mark wasn't onboard, not at first, until I really explained things to him.

We were missing it. It was right there, and we missed it.

I asked him what we were doing.

When deep inside I knew the answer.

Nothing. We were doing nothing major.

Despite our efforts, nothing we did mattered because we didn't have a purpose other than surviving, for doing it.

Was surviving enough?

Little by little we took steps to live. From the bridge, to the bus, to the basement.

Baby steps.

We left the basement to go to the hospital, then set our sights on leaving the area.

To do what? Find a place? What kind of place? Would we know when we found it?

Nothing that we did was long term visionary. It was all immediate, next step things.

There was a reason for that. There really wasn't a big picture. The big picture was wiped out by a few thousand nukes that left a devastated, yet clean slate.

The world before defined who we were because of what we did in society.

No longer did I wait tables, Mark didn't do his retired cop stuff, Joan didn't counsel.

Each and every day before the bombs, we woke up with a purpose. One outlined to us by our daily regimented lives.

That was gone.

The was no bigger picture because there was no bigger story.

We were living in an anticlimactic world now. The bombs fell. End of story. We weren't running from danger, hurrying for a cure or looking for Utopia.

It was total nuclear annihilation. Any way you slice and diced it there was never going to be a happy ending.

We were just a group of people out there looking …. again, for only the next step.

Whether that next step was the mall or an empty camp site, it was going to be the same thing.

Day by day, getting though, surviving, looking for

something, not knowing what.

All we had left in the world was our ability to make a difference. And maybe in making a difference, we would find the purpose we desperately needed.

THIRTY-FOUR – THE PURPOSE

EPILOGUE

I remember Edward's face when I asked him if the bus was operational and if it would make a difference if twenty-five medical professionals came to the mall to help.

He thought I was joking, when he found out I wasn't, his was overjoyed.

So much so, that when Devon and the others arrived, Edward disappeared somewhere in the mall for three days.

He took a little post-apocalypse vacation.

Mark argued his case, he really wanted us to leave. We all wanted to leave, but there was a human obligation to help. We were fortunate, we were able-bodied.

Joan placed the radio call to Devon and told him about the mall situation.

They were happy not only to get out of the garage and have some place to go, but Devon used the word, 'purpose'

There were reasons for all those medical personnel to be saved, one of them was to help those people in the mall.

And the people that kept coming. They didn't stop for another week. After that it was a person a day.

I was smart about keeping Macy away from everything. She stayed in the family section, which was relatively calm. Daily she would go outside and play, but she was kept far from the sick.

I am ever grateful to God for my child's health. In a world where parents lost children, my baby was alive and healthy.

It was the one thing I knew for sure I did right.

Despite my sudden surge of care and compassion for the human race, I still was unable to bring myself to care for the sick. That was just me. Then again, they didn't need my help.

We didn't stay long at the camp. I was pleasantly surprised that Ted and Joan came with me, Mark and Macy.

One month exactly after the bombs fell, we left the Mills Mall.

We followed a map someone had made during the crisis. While the internet was still up and running, he had marked every supposed safe place in the United States. Places that weren't near targets.

The poor man was dying, he never made it to any of the safe locations.

He gave us the map asking that if we found his daughter, he had sent her to Laguardo, Tennessee, we'd tell her he tried to find her.

It was a destination, but we knew it wouldn't be our final one.

Though once again, we didn't know what we were going to do, we aimed for West Texas. It was fifty-five degrees and mid-July, we didn't want to be north when Winter set in.

Maybe along the way, we could serve more of a purpose.

We didn't find his daughter, I'd keep looking, I wrote about her in my log book.

Somewhere around that little Tennessee town we saw signs that the government was starting to re-emerge.

They wanted people to check in, do a census, find out who needed help.

Surprisingly, there were a lot of communities and towns on our journey that were doing well. Surviving and building to one day thrive.

No one really mentioned wanting the government's help. Who can blame them? We didn't want their help. I wasn't even sure I wanted the government to be up and running ever again.

Only twice did we run into trouble on the road. We handled it. The minimal trouble wasn't because there wasn't any bad, there was. We just were able to successfully avoid it. We were always given a heads up when we'd stop in a town on what roads and places to avoid.

There was a lot of destruction and death on the road, but there was a lot of life. We stopped at a lot of small towns. Most of them welcomed us, shared a meal with us and told us their stories and they heard ours.

With no rush to get anywhere, we finally arrived in Texas around September.

We holed up in a trailer at a KOA campsite and were there a week when someone from a neighboring community called Woodruff spotted our campfire.

They checked on us several times before inviting us to their town.

At that point a light snow had started to fall, and it became a dreary, gray world.

Ted was a Godsend to the town, their greenhouses were failing, and he was able to successfully save their hydroponic crops.

We dug in for the winter in Woodruff, making it our home.

A temporary one.

We had no plans to stay there forever, not that it wasn't a great place, it was. Just not ours. In the end that's what we wanted, a place to call our own.

Eventually we'd find a permanent home. A good location, one to settle in, maybe start a community like Ted suggested, growing our own food.

Eventually we would do that.

After all, we survived the odds. We were alive.

Macy was a big deciding factor on what we did and when. I needed to make a life for her. A safe one in a world that wasn't dark with death, but light with hope.

I would get there. *We* would get there.

Not with help from the government, or some leader by default.

Us. The survivors that remained.

We would do it.

We left the world in someone else's hands once before and they messed it up. Now it was up to us and it was time to do things right.

<><><><>

Thank you so much for reading this book. I had fun writing it and hope enjoyed it, as well.

Please visit my website www.jacquelinedruga.com and sign up for my mailing list for updates, freebies, new releases and giveaways. And, don't forget my new Kindle club!

Your support is invaluable to me. I welcome and respond to your feedback. Please feel free to email me at Jacqueline@jacquelinedruga.com

Manufactured by Amazon.ca
Bolton, ON